TALES FROM AFRICA

HENRY M. STANLEY

GW00480511

ALAN SUTTON
1985

First published 1893

Copyright © in this edition 1985 Alan Sutton
Publishing Limited

This edition first published in Great Britain 1985
Alan Sutton Publishing Limited
30 Brunswick Road
Gloucester GL1 1JJ

ISBN 0-86299-257-5

Printed in Great Britain

CONTENTS

"HE STEALTHILY APPROACHED FROM TREE TO TREE."

See p. 55.

TALES FROM AFRICA

THE nightly custom of gathering around the camp fire, and entertaining one another with stories, began in 1875, after Sabadu, a page of King Mtesa, had astonished his hearers with the legend of the "Blameless Priest." *

Our circle was free to all, and was frequently well attended; for when it was seen that the more accomplished narrators were suitably rewarded, and that there was a great deal of amusement to be derived, few could resist the temptation to approach and listen, unless fatigue or illness prevented them.

Many of the stories related were naturally of little value, having neither novelty nor originality; and in many cases, especially where the Zanzibaries were the narrators, the stories were mere importa-

* See "Through the Dark Continent," published by Sampson Low & Co., 1878.

tions from Asia; while others, again, were mere masks of low inclinations. I therefore had often to sit out a lengthy tale which had not a single point in it.

But whenever a real aborigine of the interior undertook to tell a tale of the old days, we were sure to hear something new and striking; the language became more quaint, and in almost every tale there was a distinct moral.

The following legends are the choicest and most curious of those that were related to me during seventeen years, and which have not been hitherto published in any of my books of travel. Faithfully as I have endeavoured to follow the unsophisticated narrators it is impossible for me to reproduce the simplicity of style with which they were given, or to describe the action which accompanied them. I take my cue from the African native. He told them with the view of pleasing his native audience, after much solicitation. He was unused to the art of public speaking, and never dreamed that he was exposing himself to criticism. He was also shy, and somewhat indolent, or tired perhaps, and would prefer listening to others rather than speak himself, but though protesting strongly that his memory was defective, and that he could not remember anything, he yielded at last for the sake of peace, and good-fellowship. As these few, now about to be published, are not wholly devoid of a certain merit as examples of Central African lore, and oral literature, I have thought it best to consider myself only as a translator and to render them into English with as direct and true a version as possible.

I begin with the Creation of Man merely for preference, and not according to the date on which it was related. The legend was delivered by Matageza, a native of the Basoko,* in December 1883. He had been an assiduous attendant at our nightly circle, but hitherto had not opened his mouth. Finally as the silence at the camp fire was getting somewhat awkward, Baruti, one of my tent-boys, was pressed to say something ; but he drew back, saying that he never was able to remember a thing that was told to him, but added he, " Matageza is clever, I have heard him tell a long legend about the making of the first man by the moon."

---

* The Basoko are a tribe occupying the right bank of the Aruwimi river from its confluence with the Congo to within a short distance of the rapids of Yambuya, and inland for a few marches.

All eyes were at once turned upon Matageza, who was toasting his feet by a little fire of his own, and there was a chorus of cries for " Matageza ! Matageza ! " He affected great reluctance to come forward, but the men, whose curiosity was aroused, would not take a denial, and some of them seized him, and dragged him with loud laughter to the seat of honour. After a good deal of urging and a promise of a fine cloth if the story was good, he cleared his throat and began the strange legend about the Creation of Man as follows.

THE CREATION OF MAN.*

IN the old, old time, all this land, and indeed all the whole earth was covered with sweet water. But the water dried up or disappeared somewhere, and the grasses, herbs, and plants began to spring up above the ground, and some grew, in the course of many moons, into trees, great and small, and the water was confined into streams and rivers, pools and lakes, and as the rain fell it kept the streams and rivers running, and the pools and lakes always fresh. There was no living thing moving upon the earth, until one day there sat by one of the pools a large Toad. How long he had lived, or how he came to exist, is not

* Republished through the courtesy of the Editor and Proprietors of the *Fortnightly Review*.

known ; it is suspected, however, that the water brought him forth out of some virtue that was in it. In the sky there was only the Moon glowing and shining—on the earth there was but this one Toad. It is said that they met and conversed together, and that one day the Moon said to him :

" I have an idea. I propose to make a man and a woman to live on the fruits of the earth, for I believe that there is rich abundance of food on it fit for such creatures."

" Nay," said the Toad, " let me make them, for I can make them fitter for the use of the earth than thou canst, for I belong to the earth, while thou belongest to the sky."

" Verily," replied the Moon, " thou hast the power to create creatures which shall have but a brief existence ; but if I make them, they will have something of my own nature ; and it is a pity that the creatures of one's own making should suffer and die. Therefore, oh, Toad, I propose to reserve the power of creation for myself, that the creatures may be endowed with perfection and enduring life."

" Ah, Moon, be not envious of the power which I share with thee, but let me have my way. I will give them forms such as I have often dreamed of. The thought is big within me, and I insist upon realising my ideas."

"An thou be so resolved, observe my words, both thou and they shall die. Thou I shall slay myself and end utterly ; and thy creatures can but follow thee, being of such frail material as thou canst give them."

"Ah, thou art angry now, but I heed thee not. I am resolved that the creatures to inhabit this earth shall be of my own creating. Attend thou to thine own empire in the sky."

Then the Moon rose and soared upward, where with his big shining face he shone upon all the world.

The Toad grew great with his conception, until it ripened and issued out in the shape of twin beings, full-grown male and female. These were the first like our kind that ever trod the earth.

The Moon beheld the event with rage, and left his place in the sky to punish the Toad, who had infringed the privilege that he had thought to reserve for himself. He came direct to Toad's pool, and stood blazingly bright over it.

"Miserable," he cried, "what hast thou done ? "

"Patience, Moon, I but exercised my right and power. It was within me to do it, and lo, the deed is done."

"Thou hast exalted thyself to be my equal in thine own esteem. Thy conceit has clouded thy wit, and obscured the memory of the warning I gave thee. Even hadst thou obtained a charter from me to attempt the task, thou couldst have done no better than thou hast done. As much as thou art inferior to me, so these will be inferior to those I could have endowed this earth with. Thy creatures are pitiful things, mere animals without sense, without the gift of perception or self-protection. They see, they breathe, they exist; their lives can be measured by one round journey of mine. Were it not out of pity for them, I would even let them die. Therefore for pity's sake I propose to improve somewhat on what thou hast done: their lives shall be lengthened, and such intelligence as malformed beings as these can contain will I endow them with, that they may have guidance through a life which with all my power must be troubled and sore. But as for thee, whilst thou exist my rage is perilous to them, therefore to save thy kin I end thee."

Saying which the Moon advanced upon Toad, and the fierce sparks from his burning face were shot forth, and fell upon the Toad until he was consumed.

The Moon then bathed in the pool, that the heat of his anger might be moderated, and the water became so heated that it was like that which is in a pot over a fire, and he stayed in it until the hissing and bubbling had subsided.

Then the Moon rose out of the pool, and sought the creatures of Toad : and when he had found them, he called them unto him, but they were afraid and hid themselves.

At this sight the Moon smiled, as you sometimes see him on fine nights, when he is a clear white, and free from stain or blurr, and he was pleased that Toad's creatures were afraid of him. " Poor things," said he, " Toad has left me much to do yet before I can make them fit to be the first of earthly creatures." Saying which he took hold of them, and bore them to the pool wherein he had bathed, and which had been the home of Toad. He held them in the water for some time, tenderly bathing them, and stroking them here and there as a potter does to his earthenware, until he had moulded them into something similar to the shape we men and women possess now. The male became distinguished by breadth of shoulder, depth of chest, larger bones, and more substantial form ; the female was slighter in chest, slimmer of waist, and the breadth and fulness of the woman was midmost of the body at the hips. Then the Moon gave them names ; the man he called Bateta, the woman Hanna, and he addressed them and said :

" Bateta, see this earth and the trees, and herbs and plants and grasses ; the whole is for thee and thy wife Hanna, and for thy children whom Hanna thy wife shall bear unto thee. I have re-made thee greatly, that thou and thine may enjoy such things as thou mayest find needful and fit. In order that thou mayest discover what things are not noxious but beneficial for thee, I have placed the faculty of discernment within thy head, which thou must exercise before thou canst become wise. The more thou prove this, the more wilt thou be able to perceive the abundance of good things the earth possesses for the creatures which are to inhabit it. I have made thee and thy wife as perfect as is necessary for the preservation and enjoyment of the term of life, which by nature of the materials the Toad made thee of must needs be short. It is in thy power to prolong or shorten it. Some things I must teach thee. I give thee first an axe. I make a fire for thee, which thou must feed from time to time with wood, and the first and most necessary utensil for daily use. Observe me while I make it for thee."

The Moon took some dark clay by the pool and mixed it with water, then kneaded it, and twisted it around until its shape was round and hollowed within, and he covered it with the embers of the fire, and baked it; and when it was ready he handed it to them.

"This vessel," continued the Moon, "is for the cooking of food. Thou wilt put water into it, and place whatsoever edible thou desirest to eat in the water. Thou wilt then place the vessel on the fire, which in time will boil the water and cook the edible. All vegetables, such as roots and bulbs, are improved in flavour and give superior nourishment by being thus cooked. It will become a serious matter for thee to know which of all the things pleasant in appearance are also pleasant for the palate. But shouldst thou be long in doubt and fearful of harm, ask and I will answer thee."

Having given the man and woman their first lesson, the Moon ascended to the sky, and from his lofty place shone upon them, and upon all the earth with a pleased expression, which comforted greatly the lonely pair.

Having watched the ascending Moon until he had reached his place in the sky, Bateta and Hanna rose and travelled on by the beautiful light which he gave them, until they came to a very large tree that had fallen. The thickness of the prostrate trunk was about twice their height. At the greater end of it there was a hole, into which they could walk without bending. Feeling a desire for sleep,

Bateta laid his fire down outside near the hollowed
entrance, cut up dry fuel, and his wife piled it on
the fire, while the flames grew brighter and lit the
interior.　Bateta took Hanna by the hand and
entered within the tree, and the two lay down
together.　But presently both complained of the
hardness of their bed, and Bateta, after pondering
awhile, rose, and going out, plucked some fresh
large leaves of a plant that grew near the fallen
tree, and returned laden with it.　He spread it
about thickly, and Hanna rolled herself on it, and
laughed gleefully as she said to Bateta that it was
soft and smooth and nice ; and opening her arms,
she cried, " Come, Bateta, and rest by my side."

Though this was the first day of their lives,
the Moon had so perfected the unfinished and poor
work of the Toad that they were both mature man
and woman.　Within a month Hanna bore twins,
of whom one was male and the other female, and
they were tiny doubles of Bateta and Hanna, which
so pleased Bateta that he ministered kindly to his
wife who, through her double charge, was prevented from doing anything else.

Thus it was that Bateta, anxious for the comfort
of his wife, and for the nourishment of his
children, sought to find choice things, but could
find little to please the dainty taste which his

wife had contracted. Whereupon, looking up to Moon with his hands uplifted, he cried out :

"OH, MOON, LIST TO THY CREATURE BATETA!"

"Oh, Moon, list to thy creature Bateta! My wife lies languishing, and she has a taste strange

to me which I cannot satisfy, and the children that
have been born unto us feed upon her body, and
her strength decreases fast.   Come down, oh,
Moon, and show me what fruit or herbs will cure
her longing."

The Moon heard Bateta's voice, and coming out
from behind the cloud with a white smiling face,
said, "It is well, Bateta; lo! I come to help
thee."

When the Moon had approached Bateta, he
showed the golden fruit of the banana--which was
the same plant whose leaves had formed the first
bed of himself and wife.

" Oh, Bateta, smell this fruit.   How likest thou
its fragrance ? "

" It is beautiful and sweet.   Oh, Moon, if it be
as wholesome for the body as it is sweet to smell,
my wife will rejoice in it."

Then the Moon peeled the banana and offered it
to Bateta, upon which he boldly ate it, and the
flavour was so pleasant that he besought permission to take one to his wife.   When Hanna had
tasted it she also appeared to enjoy it; but she
said, " Tell Moon that I need something else, for
I have no strength, and I am thinking that this
fruit will not give to me what I lose by these
children."

Bateta went out and prayed to Moon to listen to Hanna's words—which when he had heard, he said, " It was known to me that this should be, wherefore look round, Bateta, and tell me what thou seest moving yonder."

" Why, that is a buffalo."

" Rightly named," replied Moon. " And what follows it ? "

" A goat."

" Good again. And what next ? "

" An antelope."

" Excellent, oh, Bateta ; and what may the next be ? "

" A sheep."

" Sheep it is, truly. Now look up above the trees, and tell me what thou seest soaring over them."

" I see fowls and pigeons."

" Very well called, indeed," said Moon. " These I give unto thee for meat. The buffalo is strong and fierce, leave him for thy leisure ; but the goat, sheep, and fowls, shall live near thee, and shall partake of thy bounty. There are numbers in the woods which will come to thee when they are filled with their grazing and their pecking. Take any of them—either goat, sheep, or fowl—bind it, and chop its head off with thy hatchet. The blood will sink into the soil ; the meat underneath the outer skin is good for food, after being boiled or roasted over the fire. Haste now, Bateta ; it is meat thy wife craves, and she needs naught else to restore her strength. So prepare instantly and eat."

The Moon floated upward, smiling and benignant, and Bateta hastened to bind a goat, and made it ready as the Moon had advised. Hanna, after eating of the meat which was prepared by boiling, soon recovered her strength, and the children throve, and grew marvellously.

One morning Bateta walked out of his hollowed house, and lo ! a change had come over the earth. Right over the tops of the trees a great globe of shining, dazzling light looked out from the sky, and blazed white and bright over all. Things that he had seen dimly before were now more clearly revealed. By the means of the strange light hung up in the sky he saw the difference between that which the Moon gave and that new brightness which now shone out. For, without, the trees and their leaves seemed clad in a luminous coat of light, while underneath it was but a dim reflection of that which was without, and to the sight it seemed like the colder light of the Moon.

And in the cooler light that prevailed below the

foliage of the trees there were gathered hosts of new and strange creatures; some large, others of medium, and others of small size.

Astonished at these changes, he cried, " Come out, oh, Hanna, and see the strange sights without the dwelling, for verily I am amazed, and know not what has happened."

Obedient, Hanna came out with the children and stood by his side, and was equally astonished at the brightness of the light and at the numbers of creatures which in all manner of sizes and forms stood in the shade ranged around them, with their faces towards the place where they stood.

" What may this change portend, oh, Bateta ? " asked his wife.

" Nay, Hanna, I know not. All this has happened since the Moon departed from me."

" Thou must perforce call him again, Bateta, and demand the meaning of it, else I shall fear harm unto thee, and unto these children."

" Thou art right, my wife, for to discover the meaning of all this without other aid than my own wits would keep us here until we perished."

Then he lifted his voice, and cried out aloud upward, and at the sound of his voice all the creatures gathered in the shades looked upward, and cried with their voices; but the meaning of their cry, though there was an infinite variety of sound, from the round bellowing voice of the lion to the shrill squeak of the mouse, was :

" Come down unto us, oh, Moon, and explain the meaning of this great change unto us ; for thou only who madest us can guide our sense unto the right understanding of it."

When they had ended their entreaty unto the Moon, there came a voice from above, which sounded like distant thunder, saying, " Rest ye where ye stand, until the brightness of this new light shall have faded, and ye distinguish my milder light and that of the many children which have been born unto me, when I shall come unto you and explain."

Thereupon they rested, each creature in its own place, until the great brightness, and the warmth of the strange light faded and lessened, and it was observed that it disappeared from view on the opposite side to that where it had first been seen, and that immediately after at the place of its disappearance the Moon was seen, and all over the sky became visible the countless little lights which the children of the Moon gave.

Presently, after Bateta had pointed these out to Hanna and the children, the Moon shone out bland, and its face was covered with gladness, and

"THEN HE LIFTED HIS VOICE AND CRIED OUT ALOUD UPWARD."

he left the sky smiling, and floated down to the earth, and stood not far off from Bateta, in view of him and his family, and of all the creatures under the shade.

" Hearken, oh Bateta, and ye creatures of prey and pasture. A little while ago, ye have seen the beginning of the measurement of time, which shall be divided hereafter into day and night. The time that lapses between the Sun's rising and its setting shall be called day, that which shall lapse between its setting and re-rising, shall be called night. The light of the day proceeds from the Sun, but the light of the night proceeds from me and from my children the stars ; and as ye are all my creatures I have chosen that my softer light shall shine during the restful time wherein ye sleep, to recover the strength lost in the waking time ; and ye shall be daily waked for the working time by the stronger light of the Sun. This rule never-ending shall remain.

" And whereas Bateta and his wife are the first of creatures, to them, their families, and kind that shall be born unto them, shall be given pre-eminence over all creatures made, not that they are stronger, or swifter, but because to them only have I given understanding and a gift of speech to transmit it. Perfection and everlasting life had

also been given, but the taint of the Toad remains
in the system, and the result will be death,—death
to all living things, Bateta and Hanna excepted.
In the fullness of time, when their limbs refuse to
bear the burden of their bodies and their marrow
has become dry, my first-born shall return to me,
and I shall absorb them. Children shall be born
innumerable unto them, until families shall expand
into tribes, and from here, as from a spring, mankind will outflow and overspread all lands, which
are now but wild and wold, ay, even to the farthest
edge of the earth.

"And hearken, oh Bateta, the beasts which thou
seest, have sprung from the ashes of the Toad. On
the day that he measured his power against mine,
and he was consumed by my fire, there was one drop
of juice left in his head. It was a life-germ which
soon grew into another toad. Though not equal in
power to the parent toad, thou seest what he has
done. Yonder beasts of prey and pasture and fowls
are his work. As fast as they were conceived by
him, and uncouth and ungainly they were, I dipped
them into Toad's Pool, and perfected them out-
wardly, according to their uses, and, as thou seest,
each specimen has its mate. Whereas, both thou
and they alike have the acrid poison of the toad,
thou from the parent, they in a greater measure

from the child toad, the mortal taint when ripe
will end both man and beast. No understanding
nor gift of speech have been given to them, and
they are as inferior to thyself as the child toad was
to the parent toad. Wherefore, such qualities as
thou mayest discover in them, thou mayest employ
in thy services. Meantime, let them go out each
to its own feeding-ground, lair, or covert, and grow
and multiply, until the generations descending from
thee shall have need for them. Enough for thee,
with the bounties of the forest, jungle, and plain,
are the goats, sheep, and fowls. At thy leisure,
Bateta, thou mayest strike and eat such beasts as
thou seest akin in custom to these that will feed
from thy hand. The waters abound in fish that
are thine at thy need, the air swarms with birds
which are also thine, as thy understanding will
direct thee.

" Thou wilt be wise to plant all such edibles
as thou mayest discover pleasing to the palate
and agreeable to thy body, but be not rash in
assuming that all things pleasant to the eye are
grateful to thy inwards.

" So long as thou and Hanna are on the earth, I
promise thee my aid and council; and what I tell
thee and thy wife thou wilt do well to teach thy
children, that the memory of useful things be not

forgotten—for after I take thee to myself, I come no more to visit man. Enter thy house now, for it is a time, as I have told thee, for rest and sleep. At the shining of the greater light, thou wilt waken for active life and work, and family care and joys. The beasts shall also wander each to his home in the earth, on the tops of the trees, in the bush, or in the cavern. Fare thee well, Bateta, and have kindly care for thy wife Hanna and the children."

The Moon ended his speech, and floated upward, radiant and gracious, until he rested in his place in the sky, and all the children of the Moon twinkled for joy and gladness so brightly, as the parent of the world entered his house, that all the heavens for a short time seemed burning. Then the Moon drew over him his cloudy cloak, and the little children of the Moon seemed to get drowsy, for they twinkled dimly, and then a darkness fell over all the earth, and in the darkness man and beast retired, each to his own place, according as the moon had directed.

A second time Bateta waked from sleep, and walked out to wonder at the intense brightness of the burning light that made the day. Then he looked around him, and his eyes rested upon a noble flock of goats and sheep, all of whom bleated their morning welcome, while the younglings pranced about in delight, and after curveting around, expressed in little bleats the joy they felt at seeing their chief Bateta. His attention was also called to the domestic fowls ; there were red and white and spotted cocks, and as many coloured hens, each with its own brood of chicks. The hens trotted up to their master—cluck, cluck, clucking— the tiny chicks, following each its own mother-- cheep, cheep, cheeping—while the cocks threw out their breasts and strutted grandly behind, and crowed with their trumpet throats, "All hail, master."

Then the morning wind rose and swayed the trees, plants, and grasses, and their tops bending before it bowed their salutes to the new king of the earth, and thus it was that man knew that his reign over all was acknowledged.

A few months afterwards, another double birth occurred, and a few months later there was still another, and Bateta remembered the number of months that intervened between each event, and knew that it would be a regular custom for all time. At the end of the eighteenth year, he permitted his first-born to choose a wife, and when his other children grew up he likewise allowed them to select their wives. At the end of ninety years, Hanna had borne to Bateta, two hundred and forty-two children, and there were grandchildren, and great-

grandchildren, and countless great-great-grand-
children, and they lived to an age many times the

"THE MOON CAME DOWN TO THE EARTH . . . AND BORE
THEM TO HIMSELF."

length of the greatest age amongst us now-a-
days. When they were so old that it became a

trouble to them to live, the Moon came down to the earth as he had promised, and bore them to himself, and soon after the first-born twins died and were buried in the earth, and after that the deaths were many and more frequent. People ceased to live as long as their parents had done, for sickness, dissensions, wars, famines, accidents ended them and cut their days short, until they at last forgot how to live long, and cared not to think how their days might be prolonged. And it has happened after this manner down to us who now live. The whole earth has become filled with mankind, but the dead that are gone and forgotten are far greater in number than those now alive upon the earth.

"Ye see now, my friends, what mischief the Toad did unto all mankind. Had his conceit been less, and had he waited a little, the good Moon would have conceived us of a nobler kind than we now are, and the taint of the Toad had not cursed man. Wherefore abandon headstrong ways, and give not way to rashness, but pay good heed to the wise and old, lest ye taint in like manner the people, and cause the innocent, the young, and the weak to suffer. I have spoken my say. If ye have heard aught displeasing, remember I but tell the tale as it was told unto me."

"Taking it as a mere story," said Baraka, " it is

very well told, but I should like to know why the
Moon did not teach Bateta the value of manioc,
since he took the trouble to tell him about the
banana."

"For the reason," answered Matageza, "that
when he showed him the banana, there was no one
but the Moon could have done so. But after the
Moon had given goats and sheep and fowls for his
companions, his own lively intelligence was sufficient to teach Bateta many things. The goats
became great pets of Bateta, and used to follow
him about. He observed that there was a certain
plant to which the goats flocked with great greed,
to feed upon the tops until their bellies became
round and large with it. One day the idea came
to him that if the goats could feed so freely upon
it without harm, that it might be also harmless
to him. Whereupon he pulled the plant up and
carried it home. While he was chopping up the
tops for the pot his pet goats tried to eat the tuber
which was the root, and he tried that also. He
cut up both leaves and root and cooked them, and
after tasting them he found them exceedingly
good and palatable, and thenceforward manioc
became a daily food to him and his family, and
from them to his children's children, and so on
down to us."

" Verily, that is of great interest. Why did you not put that in the story ? "

" Because the story would then have no end. I would have to tell you of the sweet potato, and the tomato, of the pumpkin, of the millet that was discovered by the fowls, and of the palm-oil nut that was discovered by the dog."

" Ah, yes, tell us how a dog could have shown the uses of the palm-oil nut."

" It is very simple. Bateta coaxed a dog to live with him because he found that the dog preferred to sit on his haunches and wait for the bones that his family threw aside after the meal was over, rather than hunt for himself like other flesh-eating beasts. One day Bateta walked out into the woods, and his dog followed him. After a long walk Bateta rested at the foot of the straight tall tree called the palm, and there were a great many nuts lying on the ground, which perhaps the monkeys or the wind had thrown down. The dog after smelling them lay down and began to eat them, and though Bateta was afraid he would hurt himself, he allowed him to have his own way, and he did not see that they harmed him at all, but that he seemed as fond as ever of them. By thinking of this he conceived that they would be no harm to him ; and after cooking them, he found that their fat improved the flavour of his vegetables, hence the custom came down to us. Indeed, the knowledge of most things that we know to-day as edibles came down to us through the observation of animals by our earliest fathers. What those of old knew not was found out later through stress of hunger, while men were lost in the bushy wilds."

When at last we rose to retire to our tents and huts, the greater number of our party felt the sorrowful conviction that the Toad had imparted to all mankind an incurable taint, and that we poor wayfarers, in particular, were cursed with an excess of it, in consequence of which both Toad and tadpole were heartily abused by all.

THE GOAT, THE LION, AND THE
SERPENT.

BARUTI, which trans-
lated means " gun-
powder," envied
Matageza the
" piece " of a dozen
gay handkerchiefs,
with which he had
been rewarded for
his excellent story, and one evening while he served
dinner, ventured to tell me that he also remembered a story that had been told to him when a
child among the Basoko.

" Very well, Baruti," I replied, " we will all meet
to-night around the camp fire as usual, and according to the merits of your story you will surely be
rewarded. If it is better than Matageza's, you
shall have a still finer piece of cloth ; if it is not so
interesting, you cannot expect so much."

" All right, sir. Business is business, and
nothing for him that can say nothing."

Soon after the darkness had fallen, the captains of the expedition and the more intelligent men began to form the evening circle, and after we had discussed the state of the night, and the events of the day, I called out to Baruti for his story, when, after telling us what a great time had elapsed since he had heard it, and how by searching into the recesses of his memory he had at last remembered it, he delivered the story of "The Goat, the Lion, and the Serpent," in the following manner :—

A Goat and a Lion were travelling together one day on the outskirts of a forest, at the end of which there was a community of mankind comfortably hutted within a village, which was fenced round with tall and pointed stakes. The Goat said to the Lion :

"Well, now, my friend, where do you come from this day ?"

"I have come from a feast that I have given many friends of mine—to the leopard, hyena, wolf, jackal, wild cat, buffalo, zebra, and many more. The long-necked giraffe and dew-lapped eland were also there, as well as the springing antelope."

"That is grand company you keep, indeed," said the Goat, with a sigh. "As for poor me, I am alone. No one cares for me very much, but I find abundance of grass and sweet leafage, and when I am full, I seek a soft spot under a tree, and chew my cud, dreamily and contentedly. And of other sorrows, save an occasional pang of hunger, in my wanderings I know of none."

" Do you mean to say that you do not envy me my regal dignity and strength ? "

" I do not indeed, because as yet I have been ignorant of them."

" What ? Know you not that I am the strongest of all who dwell in the forest or wilderness ? that when I roar all who hear me bow down their heads, and shrink in fear ? "

" Indeed, I do not know all this, nor am I very sure that you are not deceiving yourself, because I know many whose offensive powers are much more dangerous, my friend, than yours. True your teeth are large, and your claws are sharp, and your roar is loud enough, and your appearance is imposing. Still, I know a tiny thing in these woods that is much more to be dreaded than you are ; and I think if you matched yourself against it in a contest, that same tiny thing would become victor."

" Bah ! " said the Lion, impatiently, " you anger me. Why, even to-day all who were at the feast acknowledged that they were but feeble creatures compared with me : and you will own that if I but clawed you once there would be no life left in you."

" What you say in regard to me is true enough, and, as I said before, I do not pretend to the possession of strength. But this tiny thing that I know of is not likely to have been at your feast."

" What may this tiny thing be that is so dreadful ? " asked the Lion, sneeringly.

" The Serpent," answered the Goat, chewing his cud with an indifferent air.

" The Serpent ! " said the Lion, astounded. " What, that crawling reptile, which feeds on mice and sleeping birds—that soft vine-like, creeping thing that coils itself in tufts of grass, and branches of bush ? "

" Yes, that is its name and character clearly."

" Why, my weight alone would tread it flat like unto a smashed egg."

" I would not try to do so if I were you. Its fangs are sharper than your great corner teeth or claws."

" Will you match it against my strength ? "

" Yes."

" And if you lose, what will be the forfeit ? "

" If you survive the fight, I will be your slave, and you may command me for any purpose you

please. But what will you give me if you
lose ? "

" What you please."

" Well, then, I will take one hundred bunches
of bananas ; and you had better bring them here
alongside of me, before you begin."

" Where is this Serpent that will fight with
me ? "

" Close by. When you have brought the
bananas he will be here, waiting for you."

The Lion stalked proudly away to procure the
bananas, and the Goat proceeded into the bush,
where he saw Serpent drowsily coiled in many
coils on a slender branch.

" Serpent," said the Goat, " wake up. Lion is
raging for a fight with you. He has made a bet of
a hundred bananas that he will be the victor, and
I have pledged my life that you will be the strong
one ; and, hark you, obey my hints, and my life
is safe, and I shall be provided with food for at
least three moons."

" Well," said Serpent, languidly, " what is it that
you wish me to do ? "

" Take position on a bush about three cubits
high, that stands near the scene where the fight is
to take place, and when Lion is ready, raise your
crest high and boldly, and ask him to advance near

you that you may see him well, because you are
short-sighted, you know. And he, full of his
conceit and despising your slight form, will advance
towards you, unwitting of your mode of attack.
Then fasten your fangs in his eyebrows, and coil

"SERPENT, WAKE UP; LION IS RAGING FOR A FIGHT
WITH YOU."

yourself round his neck. If there is any virtue left
in your venom, poor Lion will lie stark before
long."

"And if I do this, what will you do for me?"

"I am thy servant and friend for all time."

"It is well," answered the Serpent. "Lead the
way.

Accordingly Goat led Serpent to the scene of the combat, and the latter coiled itself in position, as Goat had advised, on the leafy top of a young bush.

Presently Lion came, with a long line of servile animals, bearing one hundred bunches of bananas ; and, after dismissing them, he turned to the Goat, and said :

"Well, Goatee, where is your friend who is stronger than I am ? I feel curious to see him."

"Are you Lion ? " asked a sibilant voice from the top of a bush.

"Yes, I am ; and who are you that do not know me ? "

"I am Serpent, friend Lion, and short of sight and slow of movement. Advance nearer to me, for I see you not."

Lion uttered a loud roaring laugh, and went confidently near the Serpent—who had raised his crest and arched his neck—so near that his breath seemed to blow the slender form to a tremulous movement.

"You shake already," said Lion, mockingly.

"Yes, I shake but to strike the better, my friend," said Serpent, as he darted forward and fixed his fangs in the left eyebrow of Lion, and at the same moment its body glided round the neck of Lion, and became buried out of sight in the copious mane.

Like the pain of fire the deadly venom was felt quickly in the head and body. When it reached the heart, Lion fell down and lay still and dead.

"Well done," cried Goat, as he danced around the pile of bananas. "Provisions for three moons have I, and this doughty roarer is of no more value than a dead goat."

Goat and Serpent then vowed friendship for one another, after which Serpent said :

"Now follow me, and obey. I have a little work for you."

"Work! What work, O Serpent?"

"It is light and agreeable. If you follow that path, you will find a village of mankind. You will there proclaim to the people what I have done, and show this carcase to them. In return for this they will make much of you, and you will find abundance of food in their gardens—tender leaves of manioc and peanut, mellow bananas, and plenty of rich greens daily. True, when you are fat and a feast is to be made, they will kill you and eat you ; but, for all your kind, comfort, plenty, and warm dry housing is more agreeable than the cold damp jungle, and destruction by the feral beasts."

"Nay, neither the work nor the fate is grievous,

"FIXED HIS FANGS IN THE LEFT EYEBROW OF LION."

and I thank you, O Serpent; but for you there can be no other home than the bush and the tuft of grass, and you will always be a dreaded enemy of all who come near your resting-place."

Then they parted. The Goat went along the path, and came to the gardens of a village, where a woman was chopping fuel. Looking up she saw a creature with grand horns coming near to her, bleating. Her first impulse was to run away, but seeing, as it bleated, that it was a fodder-eating animal, with no means of offence, she plucked some manioc greens and coaxed it to her, upon which the Goat came and spoke to her.

" Follow me, for I have a strange thing to show you a little distance off."

The woman, wondering that a four-footed animal could address her in intelligible speech, followed ; and the Goat trotted gently before her to where Lion lay dead. The woman upon seeing the body stopped and asked, "What is the meaning of this ?"

The goat answered, " This was once the king of beasts ; the fear of him was upon all that lived in the woods and in the wilderness. But he too often boasted of his might, and became too proud. I therefore dared him to fight a tiny creature of the bush, and lo ! the boaster was slain."

" And how do you name the victor ? "

" The Serpent."

" Ah ! you say true.   Serpent is king over all,
except man," answered the woman.

" You are of a wise kind," answered the Goat.

" CONVEYED IT TO THE VILLAGE."

" Serpent confessed to me that man was his
superior, and sent me to you that I might become
man's creature.   Henceforth man shall feed me
with greens, tender tops of plants, and house and
protect me ; but when the feast-day comes, man

shall kill me, and eat of my flesh. These are the words of Serpent."

The woman hearkened to all Goat's words, and retained them in her memory. Then she unrobed the Lion of his furry spoil, and conveyed it to the village, where she astonished her folk with all that had happened to her. From that day to this the goat kind has remained with the families of man, and people are grateful to the Serpent for his gift to them ; for had not the Serpent commanded it to seek their presence, the Goat had remained for ever wild like the antelope, its brother.

" Well done, Baruti," cried Chowpereh. " That is a very good story, and it is very likely to be a true one too. Wallahi ! there is some sense in these pagans after all, and I had thought that their heads were very woodeny." It is needless to say that the sentiments of Chowpereh were generally shared, and that Baruti received the new dress he so well deserved.

THE QUEEN OF THE POOL.

K ASSIM was a sturdy lad from the Basoko country, and a chum of Baruti. As yet he had never related to us a legend, though he loved to sit near the fire, and listen to the tales of the days of old. This silence on his part was at last remarked, and one night he was urged by all of us to speak, because it was unfair that those who frequented our open-air club should be always ready to receive amusement, and yet refuse to contribute their share to the entertainment. This kind of argument pushed home, brought him at last to admit that he owed the party a debt in kind, and he said :

Well, friends, each man according to his nature, though there are so many men in the world they differ from one another as much as stones, no two of which are exactly alike. Here is Baruti here, who never seems to tire of speech, while I find more pleasure in watching his lips move up and down, and his tongue pop out and in, than in using my own. I cannot remember any legend, that is the truth; but I know of something which is not fiction, that occurred in our country relating to Izoka—a woman originally of Umané, the big town above Basoko. Izoka, the Queen of the Pool, as we call her, is alive now, and should you ever pass by Umané again, you may ask any of the natives if my words are true, and you will find that they will certify to what I shall now tell you.

Izoka is the daughter of a chief of Umané whose name is Uyimba, and her mother is called Twekay. One of the young warriors called Koku lifted his eyes towards her, and as he had a house of his own which was empty, he thought Izoka ought to be the one to keep his hearth warm, and be his companion while he went fishing. The idea became fixed in his mind, and he applied to her father, and the dowry was demanded; and, though it was heavy, it was paid, to ease his longing after her.

Now, Izoka was in every way fit to be a chief's wife. She was tall, slender, comely of person, her skin was like down to the touch, her kindly eyes brimmed over with pleasantness, her teeth were like white beads, and her ready laugh was such that all who heard it compared it to the sweet sounds of a flute which the perfect player loves to make before he begins a tune, and men's moods became merry when she passed them in the village. Well, she became Koku's wife, and she left her father's house to live with her husband.

At first it seemed that they were born for one another. Though Koku was no mean fisherman, his wife excelled him in every way. Where one fish came into his net, ten entered into that of Izoka, and this great success brought him abundance. His canoe returned daily loaded with fish, and on reaching home they had as much work to clean and cure the fish as they could manage. Their daily catch would have supported quite a village of people from starving. They therefore disposed of their surplus stock by bartering it for slaves, and goats, and fowls, hoes, carved paddles, and swords ; and in a short time Koku became the wealthiest among the chiefs of Umané, through the good fortune that attended Izoka in whatever she did.

Most men would have considered themselves highly favoured in having such fortunate wives, but it was not so with Koku. He became a changed man. Prosperity proved his bane. He went no more with Izoka to fish ; he seldom visited the market in her company, nor the fields where the slaves were at work, planting manioc, or weeding the plantain rows, or clearing the jungle, as he used to do. He was now always seen with his long pipe, and boozing with wretched idlers on the plantain wine purchased with his wife's industry ; and when he came home it was to storm at his wife in such a manner that she could only bow to it in silence.

When Koku was most filled with malice, he had an irritating way of disguising his spitefulness with a wicked smile, while his tongue expressed all sorts of contrary fancies. He would take delight in saying that her smooth skin was as rough as the leaf with which we polish our spear-shafts, that she was dumpy and dwarfish, that her mouth reminded him of a crocodile's, and her ears of an ape's ; her legs were crooked, and her feet were like hippopotamus hoofs, and she was scorned for even her nails, which were worn to the quick with household toil ; and he continued in this style to vex her, until at last he became persuaded that it was she who tormented him. Then he accused her of witchcraft. He said that it was by her witch's medicines that she caught so many fish, and he knew that some day she would poison him. Now, in our country this is a very serious accusation. However, she never crossed her husband's humour, but received the bitterness with closed lips. This silent habit of hers made matters worse. For the more patience she showed, the louder his accusations became, and the worse she appeared in his eyes. And indeed it is no wonder. If you make up your mind that you will see naught in a wife but faults, you become blind to everything else.

Her cooking also, according to him, was vile—there was either too much palm oil or too little in the herb-mess, there was sand in the meat of the fish, the fowls were nothing but bones, she was said to empty the chilli-pot into the stew, the house was not clean, there were snakes in his bed—and so on and so on. Then she threatened, when her tough patience quite broke down, that she would tell her father if he did not desist, which so enraged him that he took a thick stick, and beat her so cruelly that she was nearly dead. This was too much to bear from one so ungrateful, and she resolved to elope into the woods, and live apart from all mankind.

She had travelled a good two days' journey when she came in sight of a lengthy and wide pool which was fed by many springs, and bordered by tall, bending reeds; and the view of this body of

water, backed by deep woods all round, appeared
to her so pleasing that she chose a level place near
its edge for a resting-place. Then she unstrapped
her hamper and sitting down turned out the
things she had brought, and began to think of
what could be done with them. There was a
wedge-like axe which might also be used as an adze,
there were two hoes, a handy Basoko bill-hook, a
couple of small nets, a ladle, half-a-dozen small
gourds full of grains, a cooking-pot, some small
fish-knives, a bunch of tinder, a couple of fire-sticks,
a short stick of sugar-cane, two banana bulbs, a
few beads, iron bangles, and tiny copper balls. As
she looked over all these things, she smiled with
satisfaction and thought she would manage well
enough. She then went into the pool a little way
and looked searchingly in for a time, and she
smiled again, as if to say " better and better."

Now with her axe she cut a hoe-handle, and in
a short time it was ready for use. Going to the
pool-side, she commenced to make quite a large
round hole. She laboured at this until the hole
was as deep and wide as her own height; then she
plastered the bottom evenly with the mud from
the pool-bank, and after that, she made a great fire
at the bottom of the pit, and throughout the night
that followed, after a few winks of sleep, she

would rise and throw on more fuel. When the next day dawned, after breaking her fast with a few grains baked in her pot, she swept out all the fire from the well, and wherever a crack appeared in the baked bottom she filled it up carefully, and she also plastered the sides all round smoothly, and again she made a great fire in the pit, and left it to burn all that day.

While the fire was baking the bottom and walls of the well, she hid her hamper among a clump of reeds, and explored her neighbourhood. During her wanderings she found a path leading north-ward, and she noted it. She also discovered many nuts, sweet red berries, some round, others oval, and the fruit which is a delight to the elephants; and loading herself with as many of these articles as she could carry, she returned, and sat down by the mouth of the well, and refreshed herself. The last work of the day was to take out the fire, plaster up the cracks in the bottom and sides, and re-make the fire as great as ever. Her bed she made not far from it, with her axe by her side.

On the next morning she determined to follow the path she had discovered the day before, and when the sun was well-nigh at the middle of the sky, she came suddenly in view of a banana grove, whereupon she instantly retreated a little and hid

herself. When darkness had well set, she rose,
and penetrating the grove, cut down a large bunch
of bananas, with which she hurried back along the
road. When she came to a stick she had laid
across the path, she knew she was not far from
the pool, and she remained there until it was
sufficiently light to find her way to the well.

By the time she arrived at her well it was
in a perfect state, the walls being as sound
and well baked as her cooking-pot. After half-
filling it with water, she roasted a few bananas,
and made a contented meal from them. Then
taking her pot she boiled some bananas, and
with these she made a batter. She now emptied
the pot, smeared the bottom and sides of it
thickly with this sticky batter, and then tying
a vine round the pot she let it down into the
pond. As soon as it touched the ground, lo!
the minnows flocked greedily into the vessel to
feed on the batter. And on Izoka suddenly
drawing it up she brought out several score of
minnows, the spawn of catfish, and some of the
young of the bearded fish which grow to such an
immense size in our waters. The minnows she
took out and dried to serve as food, but the young
of the cat and bearded fish she dropped into her
well. She next dug a little ditch from the well

to the pool, and after making a strong and close netting of cane splinters across the mouth of the ditch, she made another narrow ditch to let a thin rillet of spring water supply the well with fresh water.

Every day she spent a little time in building a hut, in a cosy place surrounded by bush, which had only one opening; then she would go and work a little at a garden wherein she had planted the sugar-cane, which had been cut into three parts, and the two banana bulbs, and had sowed her millet, and her sesamum, and yellow corn which she had brought in the gourds, and every day she carefully fed her fish in the well. But there were three things she missed most in her loneliness, and these were the cries of an infant, the proud cluck of the hen after she lays an egg, and the bleating of a kid at her threshold. This made her think that she might replace them by something else, and she meditated long upon what it might be.

Observing that there were a number of ground-squirrels about, she thought of snares to catch them. She accordingly made loops of slender but strong vines near the roots of the trees, and across their narrow tracks in the woods. And she succeeded at last in catching a pair. With other vines rubbed over with bird-lime she caught some young parrots and wagtails, whose wing feathers she chopped off with her bill-hook. And one day, while out gathering nuts and berries for her birds, she came across a nest of the pelican, wherein were some eggs ; and these she resolved to watch until they were hatched, when she would take and rear them. She had found full occupation for her mind, in making cages for her squirrels and birds, and providing them with food, and had no time at all for grief.

Izoka, however, being very partial to the fish in her well, devoted most of her leisure to feeding them, and they became so tame, and intelligent that they understood the cooing notes of a strange song which she taught them, as though they were human beings. She fed them plentifully with banana-batter, so that in a few months they had grown into a goodly size By-and-by, they became too large for the well, and as they were perfectly tame, she took them out, and allowed them to go at large in the pool; but punctually in the early morning, and at noon and sunset, she called them to her, and gave them their daily portion of food, for by this time she had a goodly store of bananas and grain from her plantation and garden. One of the largest fish she called Munu, and he was so intelligent and trustful in his mistress's hands that he disliked going very far from the neighbourhood; and if she laid her two hands in the water, he would rest contentedly in the hollow thus formed. She had also strung her stock of shells and beads into necklaces, and had fastened them round the tails of her favourite fish.

Her other friends grew quite as tame as the fish, for all kinds of animals learn to cast off their fears of mankind in return for true kindness, and when no disturbing shocks alarm them. And in this lonely place, so sheltered by protecting woods, where the wind had scarce power to rustle the bending reed and hanging leaves, there was no noise to inspire the most timid with fright.

If you try, you can fancy this young woman Izoka sitting on the ground by the pool-side, surrounded by her friends, like a mother by her offspring. In her arms a young pelican, on one shoulder a chattering parrot, on the other a sharp-eyed squirrel, sitting on his haunches, licking his fore-feet; in her lap another playing with his bushy tail, and at her feet the wagtails, wagging friskily their hind parts and kicking up little showers of dusty soil. Between her and the pool a long-legged heron, who has long ago been snared, and has submitted to his mistress's kindness, and now stands on one leg, as though he were watching for her safety. Not far behind her is her woodland home, well stored with food and comforts, which are the products of her skill and care. Swifts and sand-martins are flying about, chasing one another merrily, and making the place ring with their pipings; the water of the pool lies level and unwrinkled, save in front of her, where the fish sometimes flop about impatient for their mistress's visit.

This was how she appeared one day to the cruel eyes of Koku her husband, who had seen the smoke of her fire as he was going by the path which led to the north. Being a woodman as well as a fisher, he had the craft of such as hunt, and he stealthily approached from tree to tree until he was so near that he could see the beady eyes of the squirrel on her shoulder, who startled her by his sudden movements. It was strange how quickly the alarm was communicated from one to another. His brother squirrel peeped from one side with his tail over his back like a crest, the parrot turned one eye towards the tree behind which Koku stood, and appeared transfixed, the heron dropped his other leg to the ground, uttered his melancholy cry, *Kwa-le*, and dropped his tail as though he would surge upward. The wagtails stopped their curtseying, the pelicans turned their long bills and laid them lazily along their backs looking fixedly at the tree; and at last Izoka, warned by all these signs of her friends, also turned her head in the same direction, but she saw no one, and as it was sunset she took her friends indoors.

Presently she came out again, and went to the pool-side with fish-food, and cooed softly to her friends in the water, and the fish rushed to her call, and crowded around her. After giving them their food, she addressed Munu, the largest fish, and said, "I am going out to-night to see if I cannot find a discarded cooking-vessel, for mine is broken. Beware of making friends with any man or woman who cannot repeat the song I taught you," and the fish replied by sweeping his tail to right and left according to his way.

Izoka, who now knew the woods by night as well as by day, proceeded on her journey, little suspecting that Koku had discovered her, and her manner of life and woodland secrets. He waited a little time, then crept to the pool-side, and repeated the song which she had sung, and immediately there was a great rush of fish towards him, at the number and size of which he was amazed. By this he perceived what chance of booty there was here for him, and he sped away to the path to the place where he had left his men, and he cried out to them, " Come, haste with me to the woods by a great pool, where I have discovered loads of fish."

His men were only too glad to obey him, and by midnight they had all arrived at the pool. After stationing them near him in a line, with their spears poised to strike, Koku sang the song of Izoka in a soft voice, and the great and small fish leapt joyfully from the depths where they were sleeping, and they thronged towards the shore, flinging themselves over each other, and they stood for awhile gazing doubtfully up at the line of men. But soon the cruel spears flew from their hands, and Munu, the pride of Izoka, was pierced by several, and was killed and dragged on land by the shafts of the weapons which had slain him. Munu was soon cut up, he and some others of his fellows, and the men, loading themselves with the meat, hastily departed.

Near morning Izoka returned to her home with a load of bananas and a cooking-vessel, and after a short rest and refreshment, she fed her friends— the ground squirrels, the young pelicans, the parrots and herons, and scattered a generous supply for the wagtails, and martins, and swifts ; then hastened with her bounties to the pool-side.

But, alas! near the water's edge there was a sight
which almost caused her to faint—there were
tracks of many feet, bruised reeds, blood, scales,
and refuse of fish.   She cooed softly to her friends;
they heard her cry, but approached slowly and

"MUNU, THE PRIDE OF IZOKA, WAS KILLED."

doubtingly.   She called out to Munu, "Munu-nu-
nu, oh, Munu, Munu, Munu;" but Munu came
not, and the others stood well away from the
shore, gazing at her reproachfully, and they would
not advance any nearer.   Perceiving that they
distrusted her, she threw herself on the ground

and wept hot tears, and wailing, "Oh! Munu, Munu, Munu, why do you doubt me?"

When Izoka's grief had somewhat subsided she followed the tracks through the woods until she came to the path, where they were much clearer, and there she discovered that those who had violated her peaceful home, had travelled towards Umané. A suspicion that her husband must have been of the number served to anger her still more, and she resolved to follow the plunderers, and endeavour to obtain justice. Swiftly she sped on the trail, and after many hours' quick travel she reached Umané after darkness had fallen. This favoured her purpose, and she was able to steal, unperceived, near to the open place in front of her husband's house, when she saw Koku and his friends feasting on fish, and heard him boast of his discovery of the fine fish in a forest pool. In her fury at his daring villainy she was nearly tempted to rush upon him and cleave his head with her bill-hook, but she controlled herself, and sat down to think. Then she made the resolution that she would go to her father and claim his protection—a privilege she might long ago have used had not her pride been wounded by the brutal treatment her person had received at the hands of Koku.

Her father's village was but a little distance away from Umané, and in a short time all the people in it were startled by hearing the shrill voice of one who was believed to be long ago dead, crying out in the darkness the names of Uyimba and Twekay. On hearing the names of their chief and his wife repeatedly called, the men seized their spears and sallied out, and discovered, to their astonishment, that the long-lost Izoka was amongst them once again, and that she was suffering from great and overpowering grief. They led her to her father's door, and called out to Uyimba and his wife Twekay to come out, and receive her, saying that it was a shame that the pride of Umané should be suffering like a slave in her father's own village. The old man and his wife hurried out, torches were lit, and Twekay soon received her weeping daughter in her arms.

In our country we are not very patient in presence of news, and as everybody wished to know Izoka's story, she was made to sit down on a shield, and tell all her adventures since she had eloped from Umané. The people listened in wonder to all the strange things that were told; but when she related the cruelty of Koku, the men rose to their feet all together, and beat their shields with their spears, and demanded the punishment

of Koku, and that Uyimba should lead them
there and then to Umané. They accordingly
proceeded in a body to the town, to Koku's house,
and as he came out in answer to the call of one of
them, to ascertain what the matter was, they fell
upon him, and bound him hand and foot, and
carrying him to their superior chief's house they
put him to his trial. Many witnesses came forward
to testify against his cruel treatment of Izoka, and
of the robbery of the fish and of the manner of
it ; and the great chief placed Koku's life in the
power of Uyimba, whose daughter he had wronged,
who at once ordered Koku to be beheaded, and his
body to be thrown into the river. The sentence
was executed at the river-side without loss of time.
The people of Umané and Uyimba's village then
demanded that, as Izoka had shown herself so
clever and good as to make birds, animals, and
fish obey her voice, some mark of popular favour
should be given to her. Whereupon the principal
chief of Umané, in the name of the tribe, ceded
to her all rights to the Forest Pool, and the
woods and all things in it round about as far as
she could travel in half a day, and also all the
property of which Koku stood possessed.

Izoka, by the favour of her tribe, thus became
owner of a large district, and mistress of many

slaves, and flocks, goats, and fowls, and all manner
of useful things for making a settlement by the
Pool. There is now a large village there, and
Izoka is well known in many lands near Umané
and Basoko as the Queen of the Pool, and at last
accounts was still living, prosperous and happy ;

"THE SENTENCE WAS EXECUTED WITHOUT LOSS OF TIME."

but she has never been known to try marriage
again.

Kassim's story was greatly applauded, and he
became at once a favourite with the Zanzibaris.
He was drawn towards the head man, and made
to sit down by him. One Zanzibari gave him a

handful of roasted pea-nuts, another gave him a roasted banana, while a third touched up the fire ; and the compliments he received were so many, that for the time, as one could see, he was quite vain. When a royal Dabwani cloth was spread out for inspection, and finally flung over his shoulders, we saw him cast a look at Baruti, which we knew to mean, " Ah, ah, Baruti, other folk can tell a story as well as you ! "

THE ELEPHANT AND THE LION.

T a camp on the Uppe Congo, in 1877, Chakanja drew near our fire as story-telling was about to begin, and was immediately beset with eager demands for a tale from him. Like a singer who always professes to have a cold before he indulges his friends with a song, Chakanja needed more than a few entreaties; but finally, after vowing that he never could remember anything, he consented to gratify us with the legend of the Elephant and the Lion.

"Well," he answered, with a deep sigh, "if I must, I must. You must know we Waganda are fond of three things—To have a nice wife, a pleasant farm, and to hear good news, or a lively story. I have heard a great many stories in my life, but unlike Kadu, my mind remembers them not. Men's heads are not the same, any more than men's hearts are alike. But I take it that a poor tale is better than none. It comes back to me like a dream, this tale of the Elephant and the Lion. I heard it first when on a visit to Gabunga's; but who can tell it like him? If you think the tale is not well told, it is my fault; but then, do not blame me too much, or I shall think I ought to blame you to-morrow when it will be your turn to amuse the party."

Now open your ears! A huge and sour-tempered elephant went and wandered in the forest. His inside was slack for want of juicy roots and succulent reeds, but his head was as full of dark thoughts as a gadfly is full of blood. As he looked this way and that, he observed a young lion asleep at the foot of a tree. He regarded him for awhile, then, as he was in a wicked mood, it came to him that he might as well kill the lion, and he accordingly rushed forward and impaled him with his tusks. He then lifted the body with his trunk, swung it about, and dashed it against the tree, and afterwards kneeled on it until it became as shapeless as a crushed banana pulp. He then laughed and said, "Ha! ha! This is a proof that I am strong. I have killed a lion, and people will say proud things of me, and will wonder at my strength."

Presently a brother elephant came up and greeted him.

"See," said the first elephant, "what I have done. It was I that killed him. I lifted him on high, and lo, he lies like a rotten banana. Do you not think that I am very strong? Come, be frank now, and give me some credit for what I have done."

Elephant No. 2 replied, "It is true that you are strong, but that was only a young lion. There are others of his kind, and I have seen them who would give you considerable trouble."

"Ho, ho!" laughed the first elephant. "Get out, stupid. You may bring his whole tribe here, and I will show you what I can do. Aye! and to your dam to boot."

"What? My own mother, too?"

"Yes. Go and fetch her if you like."

"Well, well," said No. 2, "you are far gone, there is no doubt. Fare you well."

No. 2 proceeded on his wanderings, resolved in his own mind that if he had an opportunity he would send some one to test the boaster's strength. No. 1 called out to him as he moved off—

"Away you go. Good-bye to you."

In a little while No. 2 Elephant met a lion and lioness, full grown, and splendid creatures, who turned out to be the parents of the youngster which had been slain. After a sociable chat with them, he said :

" If you go further on along the path I came you will meet a kind of game which requires killing badly. He has just mangled your cub."

Meantime Elephant No. 1, after chuckling to himself very conceitedly, proceeded to the pool near by to bathe and cool himself. At every step he went you could hear his " Ha, ha, ha ! loh ! I have killed a lion ! " While he was in the pool, spurting the water in a shower over his back, he suddenly looked up, and at the water's edge beheld a lion and lioness who were regarding him sternly.

" Well ! What do you want ? " he asked. " Why are you standing there looking at me in that way ? "

" Are you the rogue who killed our child ? " they asked.

" Perhaps I am," he answered. " Why do you want to know ? "

" Because we are in search of him. If it be you that did it, you will have to do the same to us before you leave this ground."

"Ho! ho!" laughed the elephant loudly.
"Well, hark. It was I who killed your cub.
Come now, it was I. Do you hear? And if you
do not leave here mighty quick, I shall have to
serve you both in the same way as I served him."

The lions roared aloud in their fury, and
switched their tails violently.

"Ho, ho!" laughed the elephant gaily. "This
is grand. There is no doubt I shall run soon,
they make me so skeery," and he danced round
the pool and jeered at them, then drank a great
quantity of water and blew it in a shower over
them.

The lions stirred not, but kept steadfastly
gazing at him, planning how to make their attack.

Perceiving that they were obstinate, he threw
another stream of water over the lions and then
backed into the deepest part of the pool, until
there was nothing seen of him but the tip of his
trunk. When he rose again the lions were still
watching him, and had not moved.

"Ho, ho!" he trumpeted, "still there? Wait
a little, I am coming to you." He advanced
towards the shore, but when he was close enough
the lion sire sprang into the air, and alighted on
the elephant's back, and furiously tore at the
muscles of the neck, and bit deep into the shoulder.

"WELL! WHAT DO YOU WANT?" HE ASKED.

The elephant retreated quickly into the deepest part of the pool, and submerged himself and his enemy, until the lion was compelled to abandon his back and begin to swim ashore. No sooner had the elephant felt himself relieved, than he rose to the surface, and hastily followed and seized the lion with his trunk. Despite his struggles he was pressed beneath the surface, dragged under his knees, and trodden into the mud, and in a short time the lion sire was dead.

The elephant laughed triumphantly, and cried, "Ho, ho! am I not strong, Ma Lion? Did you ever see the likes of me before? Two of you! Young Lion and Pa Lion are now killed! Come, Ma Lion, had you not better try now, just to see if you won't have better luck? Come on, old woman, just once."

The lioness fiercely answered, while she retreated from the pool, "Rest where you are. I am going to find my brother, and will be back shortly."

The elephant trumpeted his scorn of her and her kind, and seizing the carcase of her lord, flung it on shore after her, and declared his readiness to abide where he was, that he might make mash of all the lion family.

In a short time the lioness had found **her**

brother, who was a mighty fellow, and full of fight. As they advanced near the pool together, they consulted as to the best means of getting at the elephant. Then the lioness sprang forward to the edge of the pool. The elephant retreated a short

"DROVE ONE OF HIS TUSKS THROUGH HIS ADVERSARY'S BODY."

distance into deeper water. The lioness upon this crept along the pool, and pretended to lap the water. The elephant moved towards her. The lion waited his chance, and finally with a great roar, sprang upon his shoulders, and commenced tearing away at the very place which had been torn by lion sire.

The elephant backed quickly into deep water as he had done before, and submerged himself, but the lion maintained his hold and bit deeper. The elephant then sank down until there was nothing to be seen but the tip of his trunk, upon which the lion, to avoid suffocation, relaxed his hold and swam vigorously towards shore. The elephant rose up, and as the lion was stepping on shore, seized him, and drove one of his tusks through his adversary's body; but as he was in the act, the lioness sprang upon the elephant's neck, and bit and tore so furiously that he fell dead, and with his fall crushed the dying lion.

Soon after the close of the terrible combat, Elephant No. 2 came up, and discovered the lioness licking her chops and paws, and said—

"Hello, it seems there has been quite a quarrel here lately. Three lions are dead, and here lies one of my own kind, stiffening."

"Yes," replied lioness, gloomily, "the rogue elephant killed my cub while the little fellow was asleep in the woods. He then killed my husband and brother, and I killed him; but I do not think the elephant has gained much by fighting with us. I did not have much trouble in killing him.

Should you meet any friends of his, you may warn them to leave the lioness alone, or she may be tempted to make short work of them."

Elephant No. 2, though a patient person generally, was annoyed at this, and gave her a sudden kick with one of his hind feet, which sent her sprawling a good distance off, and asked—

"How do you like that, Ma Lion?"

"What do you mean by that?" demanded the enraged lioness.

"Oh, because I hate to hear so much bragging."

"Do you also wish to fight?" she asked.

"We should never talk about doing an impossible thing, Ma Lion," he answered. "I have travelled many years through these woods, and I have never fought yet. I find that when a person minds his own business he seldom comes to trouble, and when I meet one who is even stronger than myself I greet him pleasantly, and pass on, and I should advise you to do the same, Ma Lion."

"You are saucy, Elephant. It would be well for you to think upon your stupid brother there, who lies so stark under your nose, before you trouble with your insolence one who slew him."

"Well, words never yet made a plantation; it is the handling of a hoe that makes fields. See here, Ma Lion, if I talked to you all day I could

"HOW DID ALL THIS HAPPEN?"

not make you wise. I will just turn my back to you. If you will bite me, you will soon learn how weak you are."

The lioness, angered still more by the elephant's contempt, sprang at his shoulders, and clung to him, upon which he rushed at a stout tree, and pressing his shoulders against it, crushed the breath out of her body, and she ceased her struggles. When he relaxed his pressure, the body fell to the ground, and he knelt upon it, and kneaded it until every bone was broken.

While the elephant was meditatively standing over the body, and thinking what misfortunes happen to boasters, a man came along, carrying a spear, and seeing that the elephant was unaware of his presence, he thought what great luck had happened to him.

Said he, " Ah, what fine tusks he has. I shall be rich with them, and shall buy slaves and cattle, and with these I will get a wife and a farm," saying which he advanced silently, and when he was near enough, darted his spear into a place behind the shoulder.

The elephant turned around quickly, and on beholding his enemy rushed after and overtook him, and mauled him until in a few moments he was a mangled corpse.

Soon after a woman approached, and seeing four lions, one elephant, and her husband dead, she raised up her hands wonderingly and cried, " How did all this happen ? " The elephant, hearing her voice, came from behind a tree, with a spear quivering in his side, and bleeding profusely. At the sight of him the woman turned round to fly, but the elephant cried out to her, " Nay, run not, woman, for I can do you no harm. The happy days in the woods are ended for all the tribes. The memory of this scene will never be forgotten. Animals will be henceforth at constant war one with another. Lions will no more greet elephants, the buffaloes will be shy, the rhinoceroses will live apart, and man when he comes within the shadows will think of nothing else than his terrors, and he will fancy an enemy in every shadow. I am sorely wounded, for thy man stole up to my side and drove his spear into me, and soon I shall die."

When she had heard these words the woman hastened home, and all the villagers, old and young, hurried into the woods, by the pool, where they found four lions, two elephants, and one of their own tribe lying still and lifeless.

The words of the elephant have turned out to be true, for no man goes now-a-days into the silent and deserted woods but he feels as though something were haunting them, and thinks of goblinry, and starts at every sound. Out of the shadows which shift with the sun, forms seem crawling and phantoms appear to glide, and we are in a fever almost from the horrible illusions of fancy. We breathe quickly and fear to speak, for the smallest vibration in the silence would jar on our nerves. I speak the truth, for when I am in the woods near the night, there swims before my eyes a multitude of terrible things which I never see by the light of day. The flash of a fire-fly is a ghost, the chant of a frog becomes a frightful roar, the sudden piping of a bird signalises murder, and I run. No, no, no woods for me when alone.

And Chakanja rose to his feet and went to his own quarters, solemnly shaking his head. But we all smiled at Chakanja, and thought how terribly frightened he would be if any one suddenly rose from behind a dark bush and cried "Boo!" to him.

KING GUMBI AND HIS LOST DAUGHTER.

WE were all gathered about the fire as usual when Safeni, the sage coxswain, exclaimed, " See here, boys; do you not think that for once in a while it would be well to hear some legend connected with men and women? I vote that one of you who have amused us with tales of lions and leopards, should search his memory, and tell the company a brave story about some son of Adam. Come, you Katembo, have the Manyema no legends!"

" Well, yes, we have; but my ears have been so open heretofore that my tongue has almost forgotten its uses, and I fear that after the smooth and delightful tales of Kadu, you will not think

me expert in speech.   However, and if you care to
hear of it, I can give you the legend of Gumbi,
one of our kings in long-past days, and his
daughter."

" Speak, speak, Katembo," cried the company ;
" let us hear a Manyema legend to-night."

Katembo, after this 'general invitation, cleared
his throat, brought the soles of his feet nearer
the fire, and amid respectful silence spoke as
follows :—

It was believed in the olden time that if a king's
daughter had the misfortune to be guilty of ten
mistakes, she should suffer for half of them, and
her father would be punished for the rest.   Now,
King Gumbi had lately married ten wives, and
all at once this old belief of the elders about
troubles with daughters came into his head, and
he issued a command, which was to be obeyed
upon pain of death, that if any female children
should be born to him they should be thrown into
the Lualaba, and drowned, for said he, " the dead
are beyond temptation to err, and I shall escape
mischief."

To avoid the reproaches of his wives, on account
of the cruel order, the king thought he would
absent himself, and he took a large following with
him and went to visit other towns of his country.

Within a few days after his departure there were
born to him five sons and five daughters.   Four of
the female infants were at once disposed of according to the king's command ; but when the fifth
daughter was born, she was so beautiful, and had
such great eyes, and her colour was mellow, so like
a ripe banana, that the chief nurse hesitated, and
when the mother pleaded so hard for her child's
life, she made up her mind that the little infant
should be saved.   When the mother was able
to rise, the nurse hastened her away secretly by
night.

In the morning the queen found herself in a
dark forest, and being alone she began to talk to
herself, as people generally do, and a grey parrot
with a beautiful red tail came flying along, and
asked, " What is it you are saying to yourself, O
Miami ? "

She answered and said, " Ah, beautiful little
parrot, I am thinking what I ought to do to save
the life of my little child.   Tell me how I can save
her, for Gumbi wishes to destroy all his female
children ? "

The parrot replied, " I grieve for you greatly,
but I do not know.   Ask the next parrot you see,"
and he flew away.

A second parrot still more beautiful came flying

towards her, whistling and screeching merrily, and the queen lifted her voice and cried—

" Ah, little parrot, stop a bit, and tell me how I can save my sweet child's life ; for cruel Gumbi, her father, wants to kill it ? "

" Ah, mistress, I may not tell ; but there is one comes behind me who knows ; ask him," and hé also flew to his day's haunts.

Then the third parrot was seen to fly towards her, and he made the forest ring with his happy whistling, and Miami cried out again,

" Oh, stay, little parrot, and tell me in what way I can save my sweet child, for Gumbi, her father, vows he will kill it ? "

" Deliver it to me," answered the parrot. " But first let me put a small banana stalk and two pieces of sugar-cane with it, and then I shall carry it safely to its grandmamma."

The parrot relieved the queen of her child, and flew through the air, screeching merrier than before, and in a short time had laid the little princess, her banana stalk, and two pieces of sugar-cane in the lap of the grandmamma, who was sitting at the door of her house, and said—

" This bundle contains a gift from your daughter, wife of Gumbi. She bids you be careful of it, and let none out of your own family see it, lest she should be slain by the king. And to remember this day, she requests you to plant the banana stalk in your garden at one end, and at the

"DELIVER IT TO ME," ANSWERED THE PARROT.

other end the two pieces of sugar-cane, for you may need both.

"Your words are good and wise," answered granny, as she received the babe.

On opening the bundle the old woman discovered a female child, exceedingly pretty, plump,
and yellow as a ripe banana, with large black eyes,
and such smiles on its bright face that the grandmother's heart glowed with affection for it.

Many seasons came and went by.   No stranger
came round to ask questions.   The banana
flourished and grew into a grove, and each sprout
marked the passage of a season, and the sugar-
cane likewise throve prodigiously as year after
year passed and the infant grew into girl-
hood.   When the princess had bloomed into a
beautiful maiden, the grandmother had become
so old that the events of long ago appeared to
her to be like so many dreams, but she still
worshipped her child's child, cooked for her,
waited upon her, wove new grass mats for her
bed, and fine grass cloths for her dress, and
every night before she retired she washed her
dainty feet.

Then one day, before her ears were quite closed by
age, and her limbs had become too weak to bear
her about, the parrot who brought the child to her,
came and rested upon a branch near her door, and
after piping and whistling its greeting, cried out,
"The time has come.   Gumbi's daughter must
depart, and seek her father.   Furnish her with a

little drum, teach her a song to sing while she beats it, and send her forth."

Then granny purchased for her a tiny drum, and taught her a song, and when she had been fully instructed she prepared a new canoe with food—

"SENT HER AWAY DOWN THE RIVER."

from the bananas in the grove, and the plot of sugar-cane, and she made cushions from grass-cloth bags stuffed with silk-cotton floss for her to rest upon. When all was ready she embraced her grand-daughter, and with many tears sent her away down the river, with four women-servants.

Granny stood for a long time by the river bank, watching the little canoe disappear with the current, then she turned and entered the doorway, and sitting down closed her eyes, and began to think of the pleasant life she had enjoyed while serving Miami's child ; and while so doing she was so pleased that she smiled, and as she smiled she slept, and never woke again.

But the princess, as she floated down and bathed her eyes, which had smarted with her grief, began to think of all that granny had taught her, and began to sing in a fluty voice, as she beat her tiny drum—

> ' List, all you men,
> To the song I sing.
> I am Gumbi's child,
> Brought up in the wild ;
> And home I return,
> As you all will learn,
> When this my little drum
> Tells Gumbi I have come, come, come.'

The sound of her drum attracted the attention of some fishermen who were engaged with their nets, and seeing a strange canoe with only five women aboard floating down the river they drew near to it, and when they saw the beautiful princess, and noted her graceful, lithe figure clad in robes of fine grass-cloths, they were inclined to lay their hands upon her. But she sang again—

> 'I am Gumbi's child,
>   Make way for me;
> I am homeward bound,
>   Make way for me.'

Then the fishermen were afraid and did not molest her. But one desirous of being the first to carry the news to the king, and obtain favour and a reward for it, hastened away to tell him that his daughter was coming to visit him.

The news plunged King Gumbi into a state of wonder, for as he had taken such pains to destroy all female children, he could not imagine how he could be the father of a daughter.

Then he sent a quick-footed and confidential slave to inquire, who soon returned and assured him that the girl who was coming to him was his own true daughter.

Then he sent a man who had grown up with him, who knew all that had happened in his court; and he also returned and confirmed all that the slave had said.

Upon this he resolved to go himself, and when he met her he asked—

" Who art thou, child ? "

And she replied, "I am the only daughter of Gumbi."

"And who is Gumbi?"

"He is the king of this country," she replied.

"Well, but I am Gumbi myself, and how canst thou be my daughter?" he asked.

"I am the child of thy wife, Miami, and after I was born she hid me that I might not be cast into the river. I have been living with grandmamma, who nursed me, and by the number of banana stalks in her garden thou mayest tell the number of the seasons that have passed since my birth. One day she told me the time had come, and she sent me to seek my father; and I embarked in the canoe with four servants, and the river bore me to this land."

"Well," said Gumbi, "when I return home I shall question Miami, and I shall soon discover the truth of thy story; but meantime, what must I do for thee?"

"My grandmamma said that thou must sacrifice a goat to the meeting of the daughter with the father," she replied.

Then the king requested her to step on the shore, and when he saw the flash of her yellow feet, and the gleams of her body, which were like shining bright gum, and gazed on the clear, smooth features, and looked into the wondrous black eyes, Gumbi's heart melted and he was filled with pride that such a surpassingly beautiful creature should be his own daughter.

But she refused to set her feet on the shore until another goat had been sacrificed, for her grandmother had said ill-luck would befall her if these ceremonies were neglected.

Therefore the king commanded that two goats should be slain, one for the meeting with his daughter, and one to drive away ill-luck from before her in the land where she would first rest her feet.

When this had been done, she said, "Now, father, it is not meet that thy recovered daughter should soil her feet on the path to her father's house. Thou must lay a grass cloth along the ground all the way to my mother's door."

The king thereupon ordered a grass cloth to be spread along the path towards the women's quarters, but he did not mention to which doorway. His daughter then moved forward, the king by her side, until they came in view of all the king's wives, and then Gumbi cried out to them—

"One of you, I am told, is the mother of this girl. Look on her, and be not ashamed to own her, for she is as perfect as the egg. At the first sight

of her I felt like a man filled with pleasantness, so
let the mother come forward and claim her, and
let her not destroy herself with a lie."

Now all the women bent forward and longed to
say, " She is mine, she is mine ! " but Miami, who
was ill and weak, sat at the door, and said—

" MIAMI WAS ILL AND WEAK AND SAT AT THE DOOR."

" Continue the matting to my doorway, for as I
feel my heart is connected with her as by a cord,
she must be the child whom the parrot carried to
my mother with a banana stalk and two pieces of
sugar-cane."

" Yes, yes, thou must be my own mother," cried

the princess ; and when the grass cloth was laid
even to the inside of the house, she ran forward,
and folded her arms around her.

When Gumbi saw them together he said,
" Truly, equals always come together. I see now
by many things that the princess must be right.
But she will not long remain with me, I fear, for a
king's daughter cannot remain many moons without suitors."

Now though Gumbi considered it a trifle to
destroy children whom he had never seen, it never
entered into his mind to hurt Miami or the
princess. On the contrary, he was filled with a
gladness which he was never tired of talking about.
He was even prouder of his daughter, whose lovely
shape and limpid eyes so charmed him, than of all
his tall sons. He proved this by the feasts he
caused to be provided for all the people. Goats
were roasted and stewed, the fishermen brought fish
without number, the peasants came loaded with
weighty bunches of bananas, and baskets of yams,
and manioc, and pots full of beans, and vetches,
and millet and corn, and honey and palm-oil, and
as for the fowls—who could count them ? The
people also had plenty to drink of the juice of the
palm, and thus they were made to rejoice with the
king in the return of the princess.

It was soon spread throughout Manyema that no woman was like unto Gumbi's daughter for beauty. Some said that she was of the colour of a ripe banana, others that she was like fossil gum, others like a reddish oil-nut, and others again that her face was more like the colour of the moon than anything else. The effect of this reputation was to bring nearly all the young chiefs in the land as suitors for her hand. Many of them would have been pleasing to the king, but the princess was averse to them, and she caused it to be made known that she would marry none save the young chief who could produce matako (brass rods) by polishing his teeth. The king was very much amused at this, but the chiefs stared in surprise as they heard it.

The king mustered the choicest young men of the land, and he told them it was useless for any one to hope to be married to the princess unless he could drop brass rods by rubbing his teeth. Though they held it to be impossible that any one could do such a thing, yet every one of them began to rub his teeth hard, and as they did so, lo ! brass rods were seen to drop on the ground from the mouth of one of them, and the people gave a great shout for wonder at it.

The princess was then brought forward, and as

the young chief rose to his feet he continued to
rub his teeth, and the brass rods were heard to
tinkle as they fell to the ground. The marriage
was therefore duly proceeded with, and another
round of feasts followed, for the king was rich in
flocks of goats, and sheep, and in well-tilled fields
and slaves.

But after the first moon had waned and gone,
the husband said, " Come, now, let us depart, for
Gumbi's land is no home for me."

And unknown to Gumbi they prepared for
flight, and stowed their canoe with all things
needful for a long journey, and one night soon
after dark they embarked, and paddled down the
river. One day while seated on her cushions,
the princess saw a curious nut floating near the
canoe, upon which she sprang into the river to
obtain it. It eluded her grasp. She swam after
it, and the chief followed her as well as he was
able, crying out to her to return to the canoe, as
there were dangerous animals in the water. But
she paid no heed to him, and continued to swim
after the nut, until, when she had arrived opposite
a village, the princess was hailed by an old
woman, who cried, " Ho, princess, I have got
what thou seekest. See." And she held the nut
up in her hand. Then the princess stepped on

shore, and her husband made fast his canoe to the bank.

" Give it to me," demanded the princess, holding out her hand.

" There is one thing thou must do for me before thou canst obtain it."

" What is that ? " she asked.

" Thou must lay thy hands upon my bosom to cure me of my disease. Only thus canst thou have it," the old woman said.

The princess laid her hands upon her bosom, and as she did so the old woman was cured of her illness.

" Now thou mayest depart on thy journey, but remember what I tell thee. Thou and thy husband must cling close to this side of the river until thou comest abreast of an island which is in the middle of the entrance to a great lake. For the shore thou seekest is on this side. Once there thou wilt find peace and rest for many years. But if thou goest to the other side of the river thou wilt be lost, thou and thy husband."

They then re-embarked, and the river ran straight and smooth before them. After some days they discovered that the side they were on was uninhabited, and that their provisions were exhausted, but the other side was cultivated, and possessed many villages and plantations. For-

getting the advice of the old woman, they crossed
the river to the opposite shore, and they admired
the beauty of the land, and joyed in the odours
that came from the gardens and the plantations,
and they dreamily listened to the winds that
crumpled and tossed the great fronds of banana,
and fancied that they had seen no sky so blue.
And while they thus dreamed, lo! the river
current was bearing them both swiftly along, and
they saw the island which was at the entrance to
the great lake, and in an instant the beauty of the
land which had charmed them had died away, and
they now heard the thunderous booming of waters,
and saw them surging upward in great sweeps, and
one great wave curved underneath them, and they
were lifted up, up, up, and dropped down into the
roaring abyss, and neither chief nor princess was
ever seen again. They were both swallowed up in
the deep.

"Is *that* all?" asked Safeni, who had been
listening breathlessly to the story.

"That is all," replied Katembo.

"Why, what kind of a story is this, that finishes
in that way?"

"It is not mine," answered Katembo. "The
telling of it has been according to the words I
heard, and it is not good to alter a tale."

"Then what is the object of such a story?" demanded Safeni, in an irritable tone.

"Why to warn people from following their inclinations. Did not the girl find her father? Did not her father welcome her, and pardon the mother for very joy? Was not her own choice of a husband found for her? Was not the young chief fortunate in possessing such a beautiful wife? Why should they have become discontented? Why not have stayed at home instead of wandering into strange lands of which they knew nothing? Did not the old woman warn them of what would happen, and point to them how they might live in peace once again? But it was all to no purpose. We never know the value of anything until we have lost it. Ruin follows the wilful always. They left their home and took to the river, the river was not still, but moved on, and as their heads were already full of their own thoughts, they could not keep advice. But Katembo has ended."

THE STORY OF MARANDA.*

"M ASTER,"said Baruti, "I have been try- ing hard to recall some of the other legends I used to hear when I was very small, and I now recollect one, which is not very long, about Maranda, a wife of one of the Basoko warriors, called Mafala."

Maranda's father was named Sukila, and he lived in the village of Chief Busandiya. Sukila owned a fine large canoe and many paddles, which he had carved with his own hand. He possessed also several long nets which he had himself made, besides spears, knives, a store of grass-cloths, and a few slaves. He was highly respected by his countrymen, and sat by the chief's side in the council place.

* A Basoko Legend, republished from the " Fortnightly Magazine " by the courtesy of the Editor and Proprietors.

As the girl grew to be fit for marriage, Mafala thought she would suit him as a wife, and went and spoke of it to Sukila, who demanded a slave girl, six long paddles ornamented with ivory caps, six goats, as many grass-cloths as he had fingers and toes, a new shield, two axes, and two field-hoes. Mafala tried to reduce the demand, and walked backwards and forwards many times to smoke pipes with Sukila, and get him to be less exacting. But the old man knew his daughter was worth the price he had put upon her, and that if he refused Mafala, she would not remain long without a suitor. For a girl like Maranda is not often seen among the Basokos. Her limbs were round and smooth, and ended in thin, small hands and feet. The young men often spoke about Maranda's light, straight feet, and quick-lifting step. A boy's arm could easily enclose the slim waist, and the manner in which she carried her head, and the supple neck and the clear look in her eyes belonged to Maranda only.

Mafala, on the other hand, was curiously unlike her. He always seemed set on something, and the lines between the eyebrows gave him a severe face, not pleasant to see, and you always caught something in his eyes that made you think of the glitter which is in a serpent's eye.

Perhaps that was one reason why Sukila did not care to have him for his daughter's husband. At any rate, he would not abate his price one grass-cloth, and at last it was paid, and Maranda passed over from her father's house into that of her husband.

Soon after the marriage Maranda was heard to cry out, and it was whispered that she had learned much about Mafala in a few days, and that blows as from a rod had been heard. Half a moon passed away, and then all the village knew that Maranda had fled to Busandiya's house, because of her husband's ill-treatment. Now the custom in such a case is that the father keeps his daughter's dowry, and if it be true that a wife finds life with her husband too harsh to be borne, she may seek the chief's protection, and the chief may give her to another husband who will treat her properly.

But before the chief had chosen the man to whom he would give her, Mafala went to a crocodile—for it turned out that he was a Mganga, a witch-man who had dealings with reptiles on land, as well as with the monsters of the river,—and he bargained with it to catch her as she came to the river to wash, and carry her up to a certain place on the river bank where there was a tall tree with a large hole in it.

The crocodile bided his chance, and one morning, when Maranda visited the water, he seized her by the hand, and swept her on to his back, and carried her to the hiding-place in the hollow tree. He then left her there, and swam down opposite the village, and signalled to Mafala that he had performed his part of the bargain.

"SWAM DOWN OPPOSITE THE VILLAGE."

On the crocodile's departure Maranda looked about the hole, and saw that she was in a kind of pit, but a long way up the hollow narrowed like the neck of a gourd, and she could see foliage and a bit of sky. She determined to climb up, and though she scratched herself very much, she finally managed to reach the very top, and to crawl outside into the air. The tree was very large and lofty, and the branches spread out far, and they were laden with the heavy fruit of which elephants are so fond.* At first she thought that she could not starve because of so many of these big fruit ; then as they were large and heavy she conceived the idea that they might be useful to defend herself, and she collected a great number of them, and laid them in a heap over some sticks she had laid across the branches.

By-and-by Mafala came, and discovered her high up among the foliage, and after jeering at her, began to climb the tree. But when he was only half-way up, Maranda lifted one of the ponderous fruit and flung it on his head, and he fell to the ground with his senses all in a whirl and his back greatly bruised. When he recovered he begged the crocodile to help him, and he tried to climb up, but when he had ascended but a little way, Maranda dropped one of the elephant-fruit fairly on his snout, which sent him falling backwards. Mafala then begged two great serpents to ascend and bring her down, but Maranda met them with the heavy fruit one after another, and they were glad to leave her alone. Then the man departed to seek a leopard, but while he was absent Maranda, from her tree, saw a canoe on the river with two young fishermen

* The Jack-fruit.

in it, and she screamed loudly for help. The fishermen paddled close ashore and found that it was Sukila's daughter, the wife of Mafala, who was alone on a tall tree. They waited long enough to hear her story, and then returned to the village to obtain assistance.

Busandiya was much astonished to hear the fishermen's news, and forthwith sent a war-canoe full of armed men, led by the father, Sukila, to rescue her. By means of rattan-climbers they contrived to reach her, and to bring her down safely. While some of the war-party set out to discover Mafala, the others watched for the crocodile and the two serpents. In a short time the cruel man was seen and caught, and he was brought to the river-side, bound with green withes. His legs and his arms were firmly tied together, and, after the Basoko had made Maranda repeat her story from the beginning, and Sukila had told the manner of the marriage, they searched for great stones, which they fastened to his neck ; and, lifting him into the war-canoe, they paddled into the middle of the stream, where they sang a death-chant ; after which they dropped Mafala overboard and he was never heard of more. That is all there is of the story of Maranda.

THE STORY OF KITINDA AND HER WISE DOG.

ON another night Baruti, whose memory was freshened by the reward which followed a story worthy of being written in the Master's book, told us about Kitinda and her wise dog, so well indeed that by common consent he was acclaimed one of the best among the story-tellers. But it was not so well rehearsed to me while I had my pencil in hand as he had delivered it at the camp fire. It bothered him to be asked to dictate it a little slower to me, and he showed marked signs of inattention when told to repeat a sentence twice over. All I can flatter myself is that it contains the sense of what was said.

Kitinda, a woman of the Basoko, near the Aruwimi River, possessed a dog who was remarkable for his intelligence. It was said that he was so clever that strangers understood his motions as well as though he talked to them; and that Kitinda, familiar with his ways and the tones of his whines, his yelps, and his barks, could converse with him as easily as she could with her husband.

One market-day the mistress and her dog agreed to go together, and on the road she told him all she intended to do and say in disposing of her produce in exchange for other articles which she needed in her home. Her dog listened with sympathy, and then, in his own manner, he conveyed to her how great was his attachment to her, and how there never was such a friend as he could be; and he begged her that, if at any time she was in distress, she would tell him, and that he would serve her with all his might. "Only," he said, "were it not that I am afraid of the effects of being too clever, I could have served you oftener and much more than I have done."

"What do you mean?" asked Kitinda.

"Well, you know, among the Basoko, it is supposed, if one is too clever, or too lucky, or too rich, that it has come about through dealings in witchcraft, and people are burned in consequence. I do not like the idea of being burned—and therefore I have refrained often from assisting you because I feared you could not contain your surprise, and would chat about it to the villagers. Then some day, after some really remarkable act of cleverness of mine, people would say, ' Ha ! this is not a dog. No dog could have done that ! He must be a demon—or a witch in a dog's hide !' and of course they would take me and burn me."

" Why, how very unkind of you to think such things of me ! When have I chatted about you ? Indeed I have too many things to do, my house-work, my planting and marketing so occupy me, that I could not find time to gossip about my dog."

" Well, it is already notorious that I am clever, and I often tremble when strangers look at and admire me, for fear some muddle-headed fellow will fancy that he sees something else in me more than unusual intelligence. What would they say, how-ever, if they really knew how very sagacious I am. The reputation that I possess has only come through your affection for me, but I assure you that I dread this excess of affection lest it should end fatally for you and for me."

"But are you so much cleverer than you have already shown yourself? If I promise that I will never speak of you to any person again, will you help me more than you have done, if I am in distress?"

"You are a woman, and you could not prevent yourself talking if you tried ever so hard."

"Now, look you here, my dog. I vow to you that no matter what you do that is strange, I wish I may die, and that the first animal I meet may kill me if I speak a word. You shall see now that Kitinda will be as good as her word."

"Very well, I will take you at your word. I am to serve you every time you need help, and if you speak of my services to a soul, you are willing to lose your life by the first animal you may meet."

Thus they made a solemn agreement as they travelled to market.

Kitinda sold her palm oil and fowls to great advantage that day, and in exchange received sleeping-mats, a couple of carved stools, a bag of cassava flour, two large well-baked and polished crocks, a bunch of ripe bananas, a couple of good plantation hoes, and a big strong basket.

After the marketing was over she collected her purchases together and tried to put them into the basket, but the big crocks and carved stools were a sore trouble to her. She could put the flour and hoes and the bananas on top with the mats for a cover very well, but the stools and the crocks were a great difficulty.

Her dog in the meantime had been absent, and had succeeded in killing a young antelope, and had dragged it near her. He looked around and saw that the market was over, and that the people had returned to their own homes, while his mistress had been anxiously planning how to pack her property.

He heard her complain of her folly in buying such cumbersome and weighty things, and ask herself how she was to reach home with them.

Pitying her in her trouble, the dog galloped away and found a man empty-handed, before whom he fawned and whose hands he licked, and being patted he clung to his cloth with his teeth and pulled him gently along—wagging his tail and looking very amiable. He continued to do this until the man, seeing Kitinda fretting over her difficulty, understood what was wanted, and offered to carry the stools and crocks at each end of his long staff over his shoulders for a few of the ripe bananas and a lodging. His assistance was accepted with pleasure, and Kitinda was thus enabled to reach her home, and on the way was

told by the man how it was that he had happened
to return to the market-place.

Kitinda was very much tempted there and then
to dilate upon her dog's well-known cleverness, but

"HE TURNED, AND RAN INTO THE WOODS."

remembered in time her promise not to boast of
him. When, however, she reached the village, and
the housewives came out of their houses, burning
to hear the news at the market, in her eagerness to
tell this one and then the other all that had

happened to her, and all that she had seen and heard, she forgot her vow of the morning, and forthwith commenced to relate the last wonderful trick of her dog in dragging a man back to the market-place to help her when she thought that all her profit in trade would be lost, and when she was just about to smash her nice crocks in her rage.

The dog listened to her narrative, viewed the signs of wonder stealing over the women's faces, heard them call out to their husbands, saw the men advancing eagerly towards them, and look at him narrowly, heard one man exclaim, "That cannot be a dog! it is a demon within a dog's hide. He——"

But the dog had heard enough. He turned, and ran into the woods, and was never more seen in that village.

The next market-day came round, and Kitinda took some more palm oil and a few fowls, and left her home to dispose of them for some other domestic needs. When about half way, her dog came out of the wood, and after accusing her of betraying him to her stupid countrymen, thus returning evil for good, he sprang upon her and tore her to pieces.

THE STORY OF THE PRINCE WHO INSISTED ON POSSESSING THE MOON.

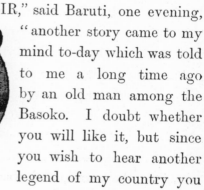

"SIR," said Baruti, one evening, "another story came to my mind to-day which was told to me a long time ago by an old man among the Basoko. I doubt whether you will like it, but since you wish to hear another legend of my country you shall have the story as it was told to me."

The country now inhabited by the Basoko tribe was formerly known as Bandimba. A king called Bahanga was its sole ruler. He possessed a houseful of wives, but all his children were unfortunately of the female sex, which he considered to be a great grievance, and of which he frequently complained. His subjects, on the other hand, were blessed with more sons than daughters, and this fact increased the king's grief, and made him envy the meanest of his subjects. One day, however, he married Bamana, the youngest daughter of his principal chief, and finally he became the father of a male child, and was very happy, and his people rejoiced in his happiness.

The prince grew up to be a marvel of strength and beauty, and his father doted on him so much, that he shared his power with the boy in a curious manner. The king reserved authority over all the married people, while the prince's subjects consisted of those not yet mated. It thus happened that the prince ruled over more people than his father, for the children, were, of course, more numerous than the parents. But with all the honour conferred upon him the prince was not happy. The more he obtained, the more he wished to possess. His eyes had but to see a thing to make him desire its exclusive possession. Each day he preferred one or more requests to his father, and because of his great love for him, the king had not the heart to refuse him anything. Indeed, he was persuaded to bestow so many gifts upon his son that he reserved scarcely anything for himself.

One day the prince was playing with the youth of his court, and after the sport retired to the shade of a tree to rest, and his companions sat down in a circle at a respectful distance from him.

He then felt a gush of pride stealing over him as he thought of his great power, at the number and variety of his treasures, and he cried out boastfully that there never was a boy so great, so rich and so favoured by his father, as he had become. " My father," said he, " can deny me nothing. I have only to ask, and it is given unto me."

Then one little slender boy with a thin voice said, " It is true, prince. Your father has been very good to you. He is a mighty king, and he is as generous as he is great. Still, I know of one thing that he cannot give you—and it is certain that you will never possess it."

" What thing is that which I may not call my own, when I see it—and what is it that is not in the king's power to give me ? " asked the prince, in a tone of annoyance.

" It is the moon," answered the little boy ; " and you must confess yourself that it is beyond the king's power to give that to you."

" Do you doubt it ? " asked the prince. " I say to you that I shall possess it, and I will go now and claim it from my father. I will not give him any peace until he gives it to me."

Now it so happens that such treasures as are already ours, we do not value so much as those which we have not yet got. So it was with this spoiled prince. The memory of the many gifts of his father faded from his mind, and their value was not to be compared with this new toy—the moon— which he had never thought of before and which he now so ardently coveted.

He found the king discussing important matters with the old men.

" Father," said he, " just now, while I was with my companions I was taunted because I did not have the moon among my toys, and it was said that it was beyond your power to give it to me. Now, prove this boy a liar, and procure the moon for me, that I may be able to show it to them, and glory in your gift."

" What is it you say, my son, you want the moon ? " asked the astonished king.

" Yes. Do get it for me at once, won't you ? "

" But, my child, the moon is a long way up. How shall we ever be able to reach it ? "

" I don't know ; but you have always been good to me, and you surely would not refuse me this favour, father ? "

" I fear, my own, that we will not be able to give you the moon."

" But, father, I must have it ; my life will not be worth living without it. How may I dare to again face my companions after my proud boast before them of your might and goodness. There was but one thing that yonder pert boy said I might not have, and that was the moon. Now my soul is bent upon possessing this moon, and you must obtain it for me or I shall die."

"Nay, my son, speak not of death. It is an ugly word, especially when connected with my prince and heir. Do you not know yet that I live only for your sake? Let your mind be at rest. I will collect all the wise men of the land together, and ask them to advise me. If they say that the moon can be reached and brought down to us, you shall have it."

Accordingly the great state drum was sounded for the general palaver, and a score of criers went through the towns beating their little drums as they went, and the messengers hastened all the wise men and elders to the presence of the king.

When all were assembled, the king announced his desire to know how the moon could be reached, and whether it could be shifted from its place in the sky and brought down to the earth, in order that he might give it to his only son the prince. If there was any wise man present who could inform him how this could be done, and would undertake to bring it to him, he would give the choicest of his daughters in marriage to him and endow him with great riches.

When the wise men heard this strange proposal, they were speechless with astonishment, as no one in the Basoko Land had ever heard of anybody mounting into the air higher than a tree, and to suppose that a person could ascend as high as the moon was, they thought, simple madness. Respect for the king, however, held them mute, though what their glances meant was very clear.

But while each man was yet looking at his neighbour in wonder, one of the wise men, who appeared to be about the youngest present, rose to his feet and said :

" Long life to the prince and to his father, the king ! We have heard the words of our king, Bahanga, and they are good. I—even I—his slave, am able to reach the moon, and to do the king's pleasure, if the king's authority will assist me."

The confident air of the man, and the ring of assurance in his voice made the other wise men, who had been so ready to believe the king and prince mad, feel shame, and they turned their faces to him curiously, more than half willing to believe that after all the thing was possible. The king also lost his puzzled look, and appeared relieved.

" Say on. How may you be able to perform what you promise ? "

"If it please the king," answered the man, boldly, "I will ascend from the top of the high mountain near the Cataract of Panga. But I shall first build a high scaffold on it, the base of which shall be as broad as the mountain top, and on that scaffold I will build another, and on the second I shall build a third, and so on and so on until my shoulder touches the moon."

"But is it possible to reach the moon in this manner?" asked the king doubtingly.

"Most certainly, if I were to erect a sufficient number of scaffolds, one above another? but it will require a vast quantity of timber, and a great army of workmen. If the king commands it, the work will be done."

"Be it so, then," said the king. "I place at your service every able-bodied man in the kingdom."

"Ah, but all the men in your kingdom are not sufficient, oh, king. All the grown-up men will be wanted to fell the trees, square the timber and bear it to the works; and every grown-up woman will be required to prepare the food for the workmen; and every boy must carry water to satisfy their thirst, and bark rope for the binding of the timbers; and every girl, big and little, must be sent to till the fields to raise cassava for food. Only in this manner can the prince obtain the moon as his toy."

"I say, then, let it be done as you think it ought to be done. All the men, women, and children in the kingdom I devote to this service, that my only son may enjoy what he desires."

Then it was proclaimed throughout the wide lands of the Bandimba that all the people should be gathered together to proceed at once with the work of obtaining the moon for the king's son. And the forest was cut down, and while some of the workmen squared the trees, others cut deep holes in the ground, to make a broad and sure base for the lower scaffold ; and the boys made thousands of rope coils to lash the timbers together out of bark, fibre of palm, and tough grass ; and the girls, big and little, hoed up the ground and planted the cassava shrubs and cuttings from the banana and the plantain, and sowed the corn ; and the women kneaded the bread and cooked the greens, and roasted green bananas for food for the workmen. And all the Bandimba people were made to slave hard every day in order that a spoiled boy might have the moon for his toy.

In a few days the first scaffolding stood up as high as the tallest trees, in a few weeks the

structure had grown until it was many arrow-
flights in height, in two months it was so lofty
that the top could not be seen with the naked eye.
The fame of the wonderful wooden tower that the
Bandimba were building was carried far and wide ;
and the friendly nations round about sent messengers to see and report to them what mad thing

"THE WOMEN KNEADED THE BREAD."

the Bandimba were about, for rumour had spread
so many contrary stories among people that
strangers did not know what to believe. Some
said it was true that all the Bandimba had
become mad ; but some of those who came to see
with their own eyes, laughed, while others began
to feel anxious. All, however, admired the
bigness, and wondered at the height of the
tower.

In the sixth month the top of the highest scaffold was so high that on the clearest day people could not see half-way up ; and it was said to be so tall that the chief engineer could tell the day he would be able to touch the moon.

The work went on, and at last the engineer passed the word down that in a few days more it would be finished. Everybody believed him, and the nations round about sent more people to be present to witness the completion of the great tower, and to observe what would happen. In all the land, and the countries adjoining it, there was found only one wise man who foresaw that if the moon was shifted out of its place what damage would happen, and that probably all those foolish people in the vicinity of the tower would be destroyed. Fearing some terrible calamity, he proposed to depart from among the Bandimba before it should be too late. He then placed his family in a canoe, and, after storing it with sufficient provisions, he embarked, and in the night he floated down the river Aruwimi and into the big river, and continued his journey night and day as fast as the current would take him—far, far below any lands known to the Bandimba.

A week later, after the flight of the wise man and his family, the chief engineer sent down

word to the king that he was ready to take the
moon down.

"It is well," replied the king from below. "I
will ascend, that I may see how you set about it."

Within twenty days the king reached the
summit of the tower, and, standing at last by the

"IN THE NIGHT FLOATED DOWN THE ARUWIMI."

side of the engineer, he laid his hand upon the
moon, and it felt exceedingly hot. Then he
commanded the engineer to proceed to take it
down. The man put a number of cool bark coils
over his shoulder and tried to dislodge it; but, as
it was firmly fixed, he used such a deal of force
that he cracked it, and there was an explosion, the

fire and sparks from which scorched him. The timber on which the king and his chiefs were standing began to burn, and many more bursting sounds were heard, and fire and melted rock ran down through the scaffolding in a steady stream, until all the woodwork was ablaze, and the flames soared upward among the uprights and trestles of the wood in one vast pile of fire ; and every man, woman, and child was utterly consumed in a moment. And the heat was so great that it affected the moon, and a large portion of it tumbled to the earth, and its glowing hot materials ran over the ground like a great river of fire, so that most of the country of the Bandimba was burnt to ashes. On those who were not smothered by the smoke, nor burnt by the fire, and who fled from before the burning river, the effect was very wonderful. Such of them as were grown up, male and female, were converted into gorillas, and all the children into different kinds of long-tailed monkeys.

The old man who told me this story ended by saying to us, who listened with open mouth to his words :

"Friends, if you doubt the truth of what I have said, all you have to do is to look at the moon when it is full, and you may then see on a

"CONVERTED INTO MONKEYS."

clear night a curious dark portion on its face, which often appears as though there were peaky mountains in it, and often the dark spots are like some kind of horned animals ; and then again, you will often fancy that on the moon you see the outlines of a man's face, but those dark spots are only the holes made in the moon by the man who forced his shoulders through it. By this you will know that I have not lied unto you. Now ever since that dreadful day when the moon burst and the Bandimba country was consumed, parents are not in the habit of granting children all they ask for, but only such things as their age and experience warn them are good for their little ones. And when little children will not be satisfied by such things, but fret and pester their parents to give them what they know will be harmful to them, then it is a custom with all wise people to take the rod to them, to drive out of their heads the wicked thoughts."

" But, Baruti," said a Zanzibari who believed the story, for had he not often viewed the dark spots on the moon, " what became of Bahanga and the little prince ? "

" Why, after the engineer of the works, the first who died were the king and the prince whose folly had brought ruin on the land."

HOW KIMYERA BECAME KING OF
UGANDA.*

K ADU was a native
lad of Uganda, who
having made blood-
brotherhood with a
young Zanzibari of
his own age, asked
permission to join
our expedition of
1874–77 He sur-
vived the perils of
the descent of the Congo, and in 1879 enlisted
again, and served faithfully another term of three
years in Africa. He afterwards joined Mr. H. H.
Johnston on his visit to Kilimanjaro, and proved
himself as devoted to him as he had been for seven
years to me. It was while road-making along the
banks of the Congo, after becoming thoroughly

* Republished from the "Fortnightly" through the kindness of its Editor and Proprietors.

conversant with the Zanzibari vernacular, that he
entertained us with his remarkable legends. Next
to his countryman Sabadu he was the most
entertaining.

One of the first tales he related to us was about
Kimyera, a king of Uganda, who by his exploits
in hunting deserves to be called the Nimrod of
that country. It ran as follows :—

Many ages ago Uni reigned as king over
Unyoro, a great country which lies to the north
and west of Uganda. One day he took to wife
Wanyana, a woman of the neighbouring kingdom,
who on the first night she had been taken into the
inner harem manifested a violent aversion for his
person. At that time a man named Kalimera, who
was a dealer in cattle, was visiting the court, and had
already resided some months there as an honoured
guest of the king, on account of his agreeable
manners, and his accomplishments on the flute.
During his stay he had not failed to note the
beauty of the young women who were permitted to
crowd around him while he played ; but it had long
been observed that he had been specially attracted
by the charms of Wanyana. It was whispered by
a few of the more maliciously disposed among the
women that a meeting had taken place, and that
an opportunity had been found by them to inform

each other of their mutual passion. However that may be, King Uni, surprised at the dislike which she manifested towards him, forbore pressing her for the time, trustfully believing that her sentiments would change for the better after a more intimate acquaintance with him. Meantime he built for her a separate apartment, and palisaded its court closely around with thick cane. His visits were paid to her on alternate days, and each time he brought some gift of bead or bark cloth, or soft, furry hide, in the hope of winning her favour.

In time she discovered that she was pregnant, and, fearing King Uni's wrath, she made a compact with him that if he would abstain from visiting her for one month she would repay his kindness with all affection. Uni gladly consented to this proposal, and confined his attentions to sending his pages with daily greetings and gifts. Meantime she endeavoured through her own servants to communicate with Kalimera, her lover, but, though no effort on her part was wanting, she could gain no news of him, except a report that soon after she had entered the harem of Uni, Kalimera had disappeared.

In a few days she was delivered of a fine male child, but as she would undoubtedly be slain by the king if the child was discovered, she departed by night with it, and laid it, clad in fur adorned with fine bead-work, at the bottom of a potter's pit. She then hastened to a soothsayer in the neighbourhood, and bribed him to contrive in some way to receive and rear her child until he could be claimed. Satisfied with his assurance that the child would be safe, Wanyana returned to her residence at the court in the same secret manner that she had left it.

Next morning Mugema, the potter, was seen passing the soothsayer's door, and was hailed by the great witch-finder.

"Mugema," said he, "thy pots are now made of rotten clay. They are not at all what they used to be. They now crumble in the hand. Tell me why is this?"

"Ah, doctor, it is just that. I thought to bribe thee to tell me, only I did not wish to disturb thee."

"It is well, Mugema; I will tell thee why. Thou hast an enemy who wishes evil to thee, but I will defeat his projects. Haste thou to thy pit, and whatever living thing thou findest there, keep and rear it kindly. While it lives thou art safe from all harm.

Wondering at this news, Mugema departed from

the soothsayer's house, and proceeded to the pit where he obtained his clay. Peering softly over the edge of the pit, he saw a bundle of bark cloth and fur. From its external appearance he could not guess what this bundle might contain, but, fearing to disturb it by any precipitate movement, he silently retreated from the pit, and sped away to tell his wife, as he was in duty bound, and obtain her advice and assistance, for the wife in all such matters is safer than the man. His wife on hearing this news cried out at him, saying :

"Why, what a fool thou art ? Why didst thou not do as the soothsayer commanded thee ? Come, I will go with thee at once, for my mind is troubled with a dream which I had last night, and this thing thou tellest me may have a weighty meaning for us both."

Mugema and his wife hurried together towards the clay-pit, and as her husband insisted on it, she crept silently to its edge to look down. At that moment the child uttered a cry and moved the clothes which covered it.

"Why, it is a babe," cried the woman ; "just as I found it in my dream. Hurry, Mugema. Descend quickly, and bring it up to me ; and take care not to hurt it."

Mugema wondered so much at his wife's words

that he almost lost his wits, but being pushed into the pit he mechanically obeyed, and brought up the bundle and its living occupant, which he handed to his wife without uttering a word.

On opening the bundle there was discovered the form of a beautiful and remarkably lusty child, of such weight, size, and form, that the woman exclaimed :

"Oh ! Mugema, was ever anybody's luck like this of ours ? My very heart sighed for a child that I could bring up to be our joy, and here the good spirits have given us the pick of all the world. Mugema, thy fortune is made."

"But whose child is it ? " asked Mugema, suspiciously.

"How can I tell thee that ? Hadst thou not brought the news to me of it being in the pit, I should have been childless all my life. The sooth-sayer who directed thee hither is a wise man. He knows the secret, I warrant him. But come, Mugema, drop these silly thoughts. What sayest thou ? shall we rear the child, or leave it here to perish ? "

"All right, wife. If it prove of joy to thee, I shall live content."

Thus it was that the child of Wanyana found foster-parents, and no woman in Unyoro could be

prouder of her child than Mugema's wife came to
be of the foundling. The milk of woman, goat, and
cow was given to him, and he throve prodigiously ;
and when Mugema asked the soothsayer what
name would be fittest for him, the wise man said :

" Call him Kimyera—the mighty one."

Some months after this, when Kimyera was
about a year old, Wanyana came to the potter's
house to purchase pots for her household, and
while she was seated in the porch selecting the
soundest among them, she heard a child crying
within.

" Ah, has thy wife had a child lately ?   I did
not observe or hear when I last visited thee that
she was likely to become a mother."

" No, princess," replied Mugema ; " that is the
cry of a child I discovered in the clay-pit about a
year ago."

Wanyana's heart gave a great jump, and for a
moment she lost all recollection of where she was.
Recovering herself with a great effort, she bade
Mugema tell her all about the incident : but while
he related the story, she was busy thinking how
she might assure herself of his secrecy if she
declared herself to be the mother of the child.

Mugema, before concluding his story, did not fail
to tell Wanyana how for a time he had suspected

his wife of having played him falsely, and that
though he had no grounds for the suspicion further
than that the clay-pit was his own and the child
had been found in it, he was not quite clear in his
mind yet, and he would be willing to slave a long
time for any person who could thoroughly disabuse
his mind of the doubt, as, with that exception,
his wife was the cleverest and best woman in
Unyoro.

Wanyana, perceiving her opportunity, said :

" Well, much as I affected not to know about the
child, I know whose child it is, and who placed it in
the pit."

" Thou, princess ! " he cried.

" Yes, and, if thou wilt take an oath upon the
great Muzimu to keep it secret, I will disclose the
name of the mother."

" Thou hast my assurance of secrecy upon the
condition that the child is not proved to be my
wife's. Whosoever else's it may be, matters not to
me ; the child was found, and is mine by right of
the finder. Now name the mother, princess."

" Wanyana ! "

" Thine ? "

" Even so. It is the offspring of fond love, and
Kalimera of Uganda is his father. The young
man belongs to one of the four royal clans of

Uganda, called the Elephant clan.   He is the
youngest son of the late king of Uganda.   To him,
on his father's death, fell his mother's portion, a
pastoral district rich in cattle not far from the
frontier of Unyoro.   It was while he drove fat herds
here for sale to Uni that he saw and loved me, and
I knew him as my lord.   Dreading the king's
anger, he fled, and I was left loveless in the power
of Uni.   One night the child was born, and in the
darkness I crept out of the king's court, and bore
the babe to thy pit.   To the wise man I confided
the secret of that birth.   Thou knowest the rest."

" Princess, my wife never appeared fairer to me
than she does now, and I owe the clear eye to thee.
Rest in peace.   My wife loves the babe, let her
nurse it until happier times, and I will guard it
safe as though it were mine own.   Ay, the babe, I
feel assured, will pay me well when he is grown.
The words of the wise man come home to me now,
and I see whereby good luck shall come to all.   If
bone and muscle can make a king, Kimyera's future
is sure.   But come in to see my wife, and to her
discretion and wisdom confide thy tale frankly."

Wanyana soon was hanging over her child, and,
amid tears of joy, she made Mugema's wife acquainted with his birth, and obtained from her
earnest assurance that he would be tenderly cared

for, and her best help in any service she could perform for Kimyera and his mother.

Great friendship sprang up between Princess Wanyana and the potter Mugema and his wife, and she found frequent excuses for visiting the fast-growing child.

Through the influence of the princess, the potter increased in riches, and his herds multiplied ; and when Kimyera was grown tall and strong, he was entrusted by his foster-father with the care of the cattle, and he gave him a number of strong youths as assistants. With these Kimyera indulged in manly games, until he became wonderfully dexterous in casting the spear, and drawing the bow, and in wrestling. His swiftness exceeded that of the fleetest antelope ; no animal of the plain could escape him when he gave chase. His courage, proved in the defence of his charge, became a proverb among all who knew him. If the cry of the herdsman warned him that a beast sought to prey upon the cattle, Kimyera never lost time to put himself in front, and, with spear and arrow, he often became victor.

With the pride becoming the possessor of so many admirable qualities, he would drive his herds right through the corn-fields of the villagers, and to all remonstrances he simply replied that the herds

belonged to Wanyana, favourite wife of Uni. The
people belonged to her also, as well as their corn,
and who could object to Wanyana's cattle eating
Wanyana's corn ? "

As his reputation for strength and courage was
well known, the villagers then submissively permitted him to do as he listed.

As he grew up in might and valour, Uni's
regards cooled towards Wanyana, and, as she was
not permitted that freedom formerly enjoyed by
her, her visits to Kimyera ceased. Mugema sympathised with the mother, and contrived to send
Kimyera with pots to sell to the people of the
court, with strict charge to discover every piece
of news relating to the Princess Wanyana. The
mother's heart dilated with pride every time she
saw her son, and she contrived in various ways to
lengthen the interview. And each time he returned
to his home he carried away some gift from Wanyana, such as leopard-skins, strings of beast claws,
beads and crocodile-teeth, girdles of white monkey-
skin, parcels of ground ochre, or camwood, or rare
shells, to show Mugema and his wife. And often
he used to say, "Wanyana bade me ask you to
accept this gift from her as a token of her esteem,"
showing them similar articles.

His mother's presents to him in a short time

enabled him to purchase two fine large dogs—one was black as charcoal, which was named by him *Msigissa*, or "Darkness," the other was white as a cotton tuft, and called *Sema-gimbi*, or "Wood-burr." You must know that it is because of the dog Darkness, that the Baboon clan of Uganda became so attached to black dogs, and perpetuate the memory of Kimyera.

When he had become the owner of Darkness and Wood-burr, he began to absent himself from home for longer periods, leaving the herds in charge of the herdsmen. With these he explored the plains, and hills, and woods to a great distance from his home. Sometimes he would be absent for weeks, causing great anxiety to his kind foster-parents. The further he went the more grew his passion to know what lay beyond the furthest ridge he saw, which, when discovered, he would be again tempted to explore another that loomed in the far distance before him. With every man he met he entered into conversation, and obtained a various knowledge of things of interest relating to the country, the people, and the chiefs. In this manner before many months he had a wide knowledge of every road and river, village and tribe, in the neighbouring lands.

On his return from these daring excursions, he

would be strictly questioned by Mugema and his wife as to what he had been doing, but he evaded giving the entire truth by rehearsing the hunting incidents that attended his wanderings, so that they knew not the lands he had seen, nor the distances that he travelled. However, being uneasy in their minds they communicated to Wanyana all that was related to them and all they suspected. Wanyana then sought permission to pay a visit to the potter and his wife, and during the visit she asked Kimyera, " Pray tell me, my son, whither dost thou travel on these long journeys of thine to seek for game ? "

" Oh ! I travel far through woods, and over grassy hills and plains."

" But is it in the direction of sunrise, or sunset, is it north or is it south of here ? "

To which he replied : " I seek game generally in the direction whence the sun rises."

" Ah ! " said Wanyana. " In that way lies Ganda, where thy father lives, and whence he came in former days to exchange cattle for salt and hoes."

" My father ! What may be my father's name, mother ? "

" Kalimera."

" And where did he live ? "

" His village is called Willimera, and is near the town of Bakka."

" Bakka ! I know the town, for in some of my journeys I entered a long way into Uganda, and have chased the leopard in the woods that border the stream called Myanja, and over the plains beyond the river many an antelope has fallen a victim to my spear."

" It is scarcely credible, my son."

" Nay, but it is true, mother."

" Then thou must have been near Willimera in that case, and it is a pity that thou shouldst not have seen thy father, and been received by him."

A few days later Kimyera slung his knitted haversack over his shoulder, and with shield, two spears, and his faithful dogs Darkness and Wood-burr, he strode out of the potter's house, and set his face once more towards the Myanja river. At the first village across the stream he questioned the natives if they knew Willimera, and was told that it was but eight hours east. The next day he arrived, and travelled round the village, and rested that night at the house of one of the herdsmen of Kalimera. He made himself very agreeable to his host, and from him he received the fullest information of all matters relating to his father.

The next day he began his return to Unyoro,

which he reached in two weeks. He told Mugema and his foster-mother of his success, and they sent a messenger to apprise Wanyana that Kimyera had returned home.

Wanyana, impatient to learn the news, arrived

KIMYERA SETTING OUT FOR UGANDA.

that night at Mugema's house, and implored Kimyera to tell her all that he had heard and seen.

"In brief, it is this," replied Kimyera. "I now know to a certainty where Kalimera lives. I have gone round the village, I know how many natives are in it, how many herds of cattle, and how many

herdsmen and slaves he has. Kalimera is well.
All these I learned from one of his chief herdsmen
with whom I rested a night. I came here straight
to let thee and my foster-parents know it."

"It is very well, my son. Now Mugema, it is
time to move," she said to the potter. "Uni daily
becomes more intolerable to me. I never have
yet mated with him as his wife, and I have been
true to the one man who seemed to me to be the
comeliest of his kind. Now that I know Kalimera
lives, my heart has gone to him, though my body
is here, Mugema, speak, my friend."

"Wanyana, my wit is slow and my tongue is
heavy. Thou knowest my circumstances. I have
one wife, but many cattle. The two cows, Namala
and Nakaombeh, which thou gavest me at first, I
possess still. Their milk has always been abundant
and sweet. Namala has sufficed to nourish Kimyera
into perfect lustiness and strength; Nakaombeh
gives more than will feed my wife and me. Let
Kimyera take his flute, his dogs, Darkness and
Wood-burr, his spears and shield; Sebarija, my
cowherd, who taught Kimyera the flute, will also
take his flute and staff, and drive Namala and
Nakaombeh. My wife will carry a few furs, some
of the spoils won by Kimyera's prowess; and, lo!
I and my family will follow Wanyana."

" A true friend thou hast been to me and mine, Mugema ! We will hence before dawn. In Willimera thou shalt receive tenfold what thou leavest here. The foundling of the clay-pit has grown tall and strong, and at last he has found the way to his father and his father's kindred."

And as Wanyana advised, the journey was undertaken that night, and before the sun arose Wanyana, Mugema and his wife, the slave Sebarija driving the two cows, Namala and Nakaombeh, were far on their way eastward, Kimyera and his two dogs, Darkness and Wood-burr, preceding the emigrants and guiding the way.

The food they took with them sustained them for two days ; but on the third day they saw a lonely buffalo, and Kimyera, followed by Mugema and Sebarija, chased him. The buffalo was uncommonly wild, and led them a long chase, far out of sight of the two women. Then Mugema reflected that they had done wrong in thus leaving the two women alone, and called out to Sebarija to hurry back, and to look after the women and two cows. Not long after, Darkness fastened his fangs in the buffalo, until Wood-burr came up and assisted him to bring it to the ground, and there they held him until Kimyera gave him his death-stroke. The two men loaded themselves with the meat, and returned to the place where they had left, but alas! they found no traces of the two women, nor of Sebarija and the two cows.

Day after day Kimyera and Mugema hunted all around the country for news of the missing party, until, finally, to their great sorrow, they were obliged to abandon the search, and came to the conclusion that it was best for them to continue their journey and trust to chance for the knowledge they desired.

Near Ganda another buffalo was sighted by Kimyera, and, bidding Mugema remain at the first house he came to, he went after it with his dogs. The buffalo galloped far, and near noon he stood still under the shelter of a rock. Kimyera bounded to the top, and, exerting all his strength, he shot his spear clean through the back of the animal. That rock is still shown to strangers as the place where Kimyera killed the first game in Uganda, and even the place where he stood may be seen by the marks of his feet which were impressed on it. While resting on the rock he saw a woman pass near by with a gourd of water. He called out to her, and begged for a drop to allay his thirst. She smilingly complied, as the stranger was comely and his manner pleasant. They entered into conversation, during which he learned that she belonged to

Ganda, and served as maid to Queen Naku, wife
of Sebwana, and that Naku was kind to strangers,
and was famed for her hospitality to them.

"Dost thou think she will be kind to me?"
asked Kimyera. "I am a native of Unyoro, and I
am seeking a house where I may rest."

KIMYERA ASKING FOR WATER.

To which the maid replied: "It is the custom
of Naku, and, indeed, of all the princes of Ganda,
to entertain the stranger since, in the far olden
times, the first prince settled in this land in which
he was a stranger. But what may that be which
is secured in thy girdle?"

"That is a reed flute on which I imitate when

alone the songs of such birds as sound sweetest to me."

" And art thou clever at it ? " asked the maid.

" Be thou judge," he said ; and forthwith blew on his flute until the maid marvelled greatly.

When he had ended, she clapped her hands gaily and said :

" Thou wilt be more than welcome to Naku and her people.   Haste and follow me that I may show thee to her, for thy fortune is made."

" Nay.   I have a companion not far from here, and I must not lose him.   But thou mayest say thou hast met a stranger who, when he has found his friend, will present himself before Queen Naku and Sebwana before sunset."

The maid withdrew and Kimyera rose, and cutting a large portion of the meat he retraced his steps, and sought and found Mugema, to whom he told all his adventures.

After washing the stains of travel and refreshing themselves, they proceeded into the village to the residence of the queen and her consort Sebwana. Naku was prepared by the favourable reports of the maid to receive Kimyera kindly, but when she saw his noble proportions and handsome figure she became violently in love with him, and turning to Sebwana she said :

" See now, we have guests of worth and breeding. They must have travelled from a far land, for I have heard of no tribe which could boast of such a youth as this. Let us receive him and his old friend nobly. Let a house close by our own be made ready for his lodging, and let it be furnished with abundance of food, with wine* and milk, bananas and yams, water and fuel, and let nothing be lacking to show our esteem for them."

Sebwana gave orders accordingly and proceeded to select a fit house as a lodging for the guests.

Then Naku said : " I hear that thou art skilled in music. If that is the instrument in thy girdle with which thou hast delighted my maid, I should be pleased to hear thee."

" Yes, Queen Naku, it is my flute ; and if my music will delight thee, my best efforts are at thy service."

Then Kimyera, kneeling on the leopard skins placed for the convenience of himself and Mugema, took out his flute, and after one or two flourishes, poured forth such melodious sounds that Naku, unable to keep her eyes open, closed them and lay down with panting breasts, while her senses were filled as it were with dreams of happier lands, and faces of brighter people than ever she knew in real

* Banana wine.

life. As he varied the notes, so varied the gladsome visions of her mind. When the music gently vibrated on her ears, her body palpitated under the influence of the emotions which swayed her; when they became more enlivened she tossed her arms about, and laughed convulsively; and when the notes took a solemn tone, she sighed and wept as though all her friends had left her only their tender memory. Grieved that Naku should suffer, Kimyera woke the queen from her sorrowful condition with tones that soon started her to her feet, and lo, all at once, those who were present joined in the lively dance, and nothing but gay laughter was heard from them. Oh, it was wonderful what quick changes came over people as they heard the flute of Kimyera. When he ceased people began to look at one another in a foolish and confused way, as though something very strange had happened to them.

But Naku quickly recovered, and went to Kimyera, smiling and saying:

"It is for thee to command, O Kimyera. To resist thy flute would be impossible. Again welcome to Ganda, and we shall see if we cannot keep thee and thy flute amongst us."

She conducted Kimyera and his foster-father Mugema to their house. She examined carefully

the arrangements made by the slaves, and when
she found anything amiss she corrected it with her
own hands. Before she parted from them she
called Mugema aside, and questioned him further
respecting the youth, by which means she obtained
many interesting particulars concerning him.

On arriving at her own house she called all the
pages of the court to her, and gave orders that if
Sebwana told them to convey such and such things
to the strangers next day, that none of them
should do so, but carry them to the rear court
where only women were admitted.

In consequence of this command Mugema and
Kimyera found themselves deserted next day, and
not one person went near them. Mugema therefore sought an interview the day after with Queen
Naku and said :

" The custom of this country seems strange to us,
O Queen. On the first day we came thy favours
showered abundance on us, but on the next not a
single person showed his face to us. Had we been
in a wilderness we could not have been more alone.
It is possible that we may have offended thee unknown to ourselves. Pray acquaint us with our
offence, or permit us to depart at once from
Ganda."

" Nay, Mugema, I must ask thee to be patient.

Food ye shall have in abundance, through my women, and much more is in store for ye. But come, I will visit the young stranger, and thou shalt lead me to him."

Kimyera had been deep in thought ever since he had parted from Naku, and he had not observed what Mugema had complained of ; but on seeing Naku enter his house, he hasted and laid matting on the floor, and, covering it with leopard skins, begged Naku to be seated on them. He brought fresh banana-leaves in his arms, and spread them near her, on which he arranged meat and salt, and bananas and clotted milk, and kneeled before her like a ready servitor.

Naku observed all his movements, her admiration for his person and graces of body becoming stronger every minute. She peeled a mellow banana and handed it to him, saying : " Let Kimyera taste and eat with me and I will then know that I am in the house of a friend."

Kimyera accepted the gift with thanks, and ate the banana as though he had never eaten anything so delicious in his life. Then he also peeled a beautiful and ripe banana, and, presenting it to her on a fragment of green leaf with both hands, said to her :

" Queen Naku, it is the custom of my country

for the master of the house to wait upon his guests.
Wherefore accept, O Queen, this banana as a
token of friendship from the hands of Kimyera."

The queen smiled, bent forward with her eyes
fixed on his own, and took the yellow fruit, and
ate it as though such sweetness was not known in
the banana land of Ganda.

When she had eaten she said :

" List, Kimyera, and thou, Mugema, hearken
well, for I am about to utter weighty words. In
Ganda, since the death of my father, there has
been no king. Sebwana is my consort by choice
of the elders of the land, but in name only. He is
really only my *kate-kiro* (Premier). But I am now
old enough to choose a king for myself, and according to custom, I may do so. Wherefore I make
known to thee, Mugema, that I have already
chosen my lord and husband, and he by due right
must occupy the chair of my father, the old king
who is dead. I have said to myself since the day
before yesterday that my lord and husband shall
be Kimyera."

Both Kimyera and Mugema prostrated themselves three times before Naku, and, after the
youth had recovered from his confusion and
surprise, he replied :

" But, Queen Naku, hast thou thought what the

people will say to this? May it not be that they will ask, 'Who is this stranger that he should reign over us?' and they will be wroth with me and try to slay me?"

"Nay. For thou art my father's brother's son, as Mugema told me, and my father having left no male heirs of his body, his daughter may, if she choose, ally herself with a son of his brother. Kalimera is a younger brother of my father. Thou seest, therefore, that thou, Kimyera, hast a right to the king's chair, if I, Naku, will it to be so."

"And how, Naku, dost thou propose to act. In thy cause my arm is ready to strike. Thou hast but to speak."

"In this way. I will now leave thee, for I have some business for Sebwana. When he has gone I will then send for thee, and thou, when thou comest to me, must say, 'Naku, I have come. What can Kimyera do for Queen Naku?' And I will rise and say, 'Kimyera, come and seat thyself in thy father's brother's chair.' And thou wilt step forward, bow three times before me, then six times before the king's chair, and, with thy best spear in hand and shield on arm, thou wilt proceed to the king's chair, and turning to the people who will be present, say in a loud voice thus: 'Lo, people

of Ganda, I am Kimyera, son of Kalimera, by
Wanyana of Unyoro. I hereby declare that with
her own free will I this day do take Naku, my
father's brother's daughter, to wife, and seat myself
in the king's chair. Let all obey, on pain of death,
the king's word."

" It is well, Naku ; be it according to thy wish,"
replied Kimyera.

Naku departed and proceeded in search of
Sebwana ; and, when she found him, she affected
great distress and indignation.

" How is this, Sebwana ? I gave orders that
our guests should be tenderly cared for and
supplied with every needful thing. But I find, on
inquiring this morning, that all through yesterday
they were left alone to wonder at our sudden
disregard for their wants. Haste, my friend, and
make amends for thy neglect. Go to my fields
and plantations, collect all that is choicest for our
guests, lest, when they leave us, they will proclaim
our unkindness."

Sebwana was amazed at this charge of neglect,
and in anger hastened to find out the pages. But
the pages, through Naku's good care, absented
themselves, and could not be found ; so that old
Sebwana was obliged to depend upon a few
unarmed slaves to drive the cattle and carry the

choicest treasures of the queen's fields and plantations for the use of the strangers.

Sebwana having at last left the town, Naku
returned to Kimyera, whom she found with a sad
and disconsolate aspect.

"Why, what ails thee, Kimyera?" she asked.
"The chair is now vacant. Arm thyself and follow
me to the audience court."

"Ah, Naku! I but now remembered that as
yet I know not whether my mother and good
nurse are alive or dead. They may be waiting for
me anxiously somewhere near the Myanja, or their
bones may be bleaching on one of the great plains
we traversed in coming hither."

"Nay, Kimyera, my lord, this is not a time for
mourning. Bethink thee of the present needs first.
The chair of the king awaits thee. Rise, and
occupy it, and to-morrow all Ganda is at thy
service to find thy lost mother and nurse. Come,
delay not, lest Sebwana return and take vengeance
on us all."

"Fear not, Naku, it was but a passing fit of grief
which filled my mind. Sebwana must needs be
strong and brave to dispossess me when Naku is
on my side," saying which Kimyera dressed himself
in war-costume, with a crown of cock's-tail feathers
on his head, a great leopard skin depending from

his neck down his back, a girdle of white monkey skin round his waist, his body and face brilliantly painted with vermilion and saffron. He then armed himself with two bright shining spears of great length, and bearing a shield of dried elephant hide, which no ordinary spear could penetrate, he strode after Queen Naku towards the audience court in the royal palace. Mugema, somewhat similarly armed, followed his foster-son.

As Kimyera strode proudly on, the great drum of Ganda sounded, and its deep tones were heard far and wide. Immediately the populace, who knew well that the summons of the great drum announced an important event, hastily armed themselves, and filled the great court. Naku, the queen, they found seated in a chair alongside of the king's chair, which was now unfilled, and in front of her was a tall young stranger, who prostrated himself three times before the queen. He was then seen bowing six times before the empty king's chair. Rising to his feet, he stepped towards it, and afterwards faced the multitude, who were looking on wonderingly.

The young stranger, lifting his long spears and raising his shield in an attitude of defence, cried out aloud, so that all heard his voice :

" Lo, people of Ganda ! I am Kimyera, son of

KIMYERA CLAIMING THE THRONE OF GANDA.

Kalimera, by Wanyana of Unyoro. I hereby
declare that with her own free will I this day do
take Naku, my father's brother's daughter, to wife,
and seat myself in the king's chair. Let all obey,
on pain of death, the king's word."

On concluding this address, he stepped back a
pace, and gravely sat in the king's chair. A loud
murmur rose from the multitude, and the shafts of
spears were seen rising up, when Naku rose to her
feet, and said :

" People of Ganda, open your ears. I, Naku,
the legitimate queen of Ganda, hereby declare that
I have found my father's brother's son, and I, this
day, of my own free will and great love for him, do
take him for my lord and husband. By full right
Kimyera fills the king's chair. I charge you all
henceforth to be loyal to him, and him only."

As she ended her speech the people gave a great
shout of welcome to the new king, and they waved
their spears, and clashed them against their
shields, thus signifying their willing allegiance to
King Kimyera.

The next day great bodies of strong men were
despatched in different directions for the king's
mother and his nurse, and for Sebarija and the two
cows, Namala and Nakaombeh. If alive they were
instructed to convey them with honour and care to

Ganda, and if any fatal misadventure had happened to them, their remains were to be borne with all due respect to the king.

Sebwana, meanwhile, had started for the plantations, and hearing the thunder of the great drum, divined that Naku had deposed him in favour of the young stranger. To assure himself of the fact, he sent a confidential slave to discover the truth of the matter, while he sought a place where he could await, unobserved, the return of his messenger. When his slave came back to him he learned what great event had occurred during his short absence, and that his power had been given to another. Knowing the fate attending those thus deposed, he secretly retired to the district that had given him birth, where he lived obscure and safe until he died at a good old age.

After some days Sebarija and Mugema's wife, and the two cows Namala and Nakaombeh, were found by the banks of Myanja, near a rocky hill which contained a cave, whither they had retired to seek a dwelling-place until news could be found of Mugema and Kimyera. But Wanyana, the king's mother, while gathering fuel near the cave during the absence of Sebarija and the potter's wife, had been fatally wounded by a leopard, before her cries brought Sebarija to her rescue. A short time after she had been taken into the cave she had died of her wounds, and her body had been folded in such furs and covering as her friends possessed, that Kimyera, on his return, might be satisfied of the manner of her death.

Kimyera, accompanied by his wife Naku and old Mugema, set out from Ganda with a great escort to receive the long-lost couple and the remains of Wanyana. Mugema rejoiced to see his old wife once more, though he deeply regretted the loss of his friend the princess. As for the king, his grief was excessive, but Naku, with her loving ways, assisted him to bear his great misfortune. A period of mourning, for an entire moon, was enjoined on all the people, after which a great mound was built at Kagoma over the remains of the unfortunate princess, and Sebarija was duly installed as keeper of the monument. Ever since that day it has become the custom to bury the queen-mothers near the grave of Wanyana, and to appoint keepers of the royal cemetery in memory of Sebarija, who first occupied that post.

While he lived Sebarija was honoured with a visit, on the first day of every alternate moon, from Kimyera, who always brought with him a young buffalo as a gift to the faithful cowherd. During these days the king and Sebarija were

accustomed to play their flutes together as they
did in the old time, and their seats were on mats
placed on top of the mound, while the escort
and servants of the king and queen sat all round
the foot of it, and this was the manner in which
Wanyana's memory was honoured during her
son's life.

Kimyera finally settled with Queen Naku at
Birra, where he built a large town. Mugema and
his wife, with their two cows Namala and
Nakaombeh, lived near the palace for many years,
until they died.

Darkness and Wood-burr accompanied the king
on many a hunt in the plains bordering the Myanja,
in the woods of Ruwambo, and along the lake-
lands which look towards Bussi; and they in their
turn died and were honourably interred with many
folds of bark-cloth. Queen Naku, after giving
birth to three sons, died during the birth of her
fourth child, and was buried with great honour
near Birra, and finally, after living to a great old
age, the hunter king, Kimyera, died, mourned by
all his people.

THE LEGEND OF THE LEOPARDESS AND HER TWO SERVANTS, DOG AND JACKAL.

THE following legend was also told by Kadu as we approached Isangila cataract.

Long ago, in the early age of Uganda, a leopardess, in want of a servant to do chores in her den, was solicited by a jackal to engage him to perform that duty. As Jackal, with his ears drawn back, and his furtive eyes, and a smile which always seemed to be a leer, had a very suspicious appearance, the Leopardess consulted with Dog, whom she had lately hired as her steward, as to the propriety of trusting such a cunning-looking animal.

Dog trotted out to the entrance of the den to examine the stranger for himself, and, after close inspection of him, asked Jackal what work he could do. Jackal replied humbly and fawningly, and said that he could fetch water from the brook, collect fuel, sweep out the house, and was willing, if necessary, to cook now and then, as he was not a novice in the art of cooking; and, looking at Leopardess, "I am very fond of cubs, and am very clever in nursing them." Mistress Leopardess, on hearing this, seemed to be impressed with the abilities of Jackal, and, without waiting for the advice of Dog, engaged him at once, and said :

"Jackal, you must understand that my custom is to feed my servants well. What is left from my table is so abundant that I have heard no complaints from any who have been with me. Therefore you need fear no starvation, but while you may depend upon being supplied with plenty of meat, the bones must not be touched. Dog shall be your companion, but neither he nor anyone else is permitted to touch the bones."

"I shall be quite content, Mistress Leopardess. Meat is good enough for me, and for good meat you may depend upon it I shall give good work."

The household of Mistress Leopardess being thus

completed; she suffered no anxiety, and enjoyed herself in her own way. The chase was her great delight. The forest and plains were alive with game, and each morning at sunrise it was her custom to set out for the hunt, and scarcely a day passed but she returned with sufficient meat to satisfy her household. Dog and Jackal expressed themselves delighted with the luscious repasts which they enjoyed, and a sleek roundness witnessed that they fared nobly. But as it frequently happens with people who have everything they desire, Dog, in a short while, became more nice and fastidious in his tastes. He hankered after the bones which were forbidden him, and was heard to sigh deeply whenever Mistress Leopardess collected the bones and stored them in the interior, and his eyes became filled with tears as he eyed the rich morsels stowed away. His feelings at last becoming intolerable, he resolved to appeal to his mistress one day, when she appeared to be in a more amiable mood than usual, and said :

" Mistress, thanks to you, the house is always well supplied with meat, and none of your servants have any reason to think that they will ever suffer the pangs of hunger ; but, speaking for myself, mistress mine, I wish for one thing more, if you will be so good as to grant it."

" And what may that be, greedy one ? " asked Leopardess.

" Well, you see, mistress, I fear you do not understand the nature of dogs very well. You must know dogs delight in marrow, and often prefer it to meat. The latter by itself is good, but however plentiful and good it may be, without an occasional morsel of marrow it is apt to pall. Dogs also love to sharpen their teeth on bones and screw their tongues within the holes for the sake of the rich juice. By itself, marrow would not fatten my ribs ; but meat with marrow is most delectable. Now, good mistress, seeing that I have been so faithful in your service, so docile and prompt to do your bidding, will you not be gracious enough to let me gnaw the bones and extract the marrow ? "

" No," roared Leopardess decisively, " that is positively forbidden ; and let me warn you that the day you venture to do so, a strange event will happen suddenly, which shall have most serious consequences to you and to all in this house.

" And you, Jackal, bear what I say well in mind," she continued, turning to that servile subordinate.

" Yes, mistress ; I will, most certainly. Indeed,

I do not care very greatly for bones," said Jackal, "and I hope my friend and mate, Dog, will remember, good mistress, what you say."

"I hear, mistress," replied Dog, "and since it is your will, I must needs obey."

The alarming words of Leopardess had the effect of compelling Dog and Jackal for awhile to desist from even thinking of marrow, and the entreaty of Dog appeared to be forgotten by Leopardess, though Jackal was well aware, by the sparkles in the covetous eyes of Dog when any large bone was near him, how difficult it was for him to resist the temptation. Day after day Leopardess sallied out from her den, and returned with kids, goats, sheep, antelopes, zebra, and often a young giraffe; and one day she brought a great buffalo to her household, and cubs and servants came running to greet her, and praise her successful hunting.

On this day Dog undertook to prepare the dinner. The buffalo-meat was cooked in exquisite fashion, and when it was turned out of the great pot, steaming and trickling over everywhere with juice, Dog caught sight of a thigh-bone and yellow marrow glistening within. The temptation to steal it was too great to resist. He contrived to drop the bone back again into the pot, furnished the tray quickly with the meat, and sent Jackal

with it to Leopardess, saying that he would
follow with the kabobs and stew. As soon as
Jackal had gone out of the kitchen, Dog whipped
the bone out of the pot and slyly hid it; then,
loading stew and kabobs on a tray, he hurried
after Jackal, and began officiously bustling about,
fawning upon Leopardess, stroking the cubs as
he placed them near their mamma around the
smoking trays, scolding Jackal for his laziness, and
bidding him hurry up with the steaks. All of
which, of course, was due to his delight that he
had a rare treat in store for himself snugly hidden
away.

Leopardess was pleased to bestow a good many
praises upon Dog's cooking, and the cubs even
condescended to smile their approval for the excellent way in which their wants were supplied.

Towards evening Mistress Leopardess went out
again, but not before reminding Jackal of his
duties towards the cubs, and bidding him, if it
were late before she returned, on no account to
leave them alone in the dark. Dog smilingly
followed his mistress to the door, wishing her, in
the most fawning manner, every success. When
he thought that his mistress was far enough, and
Jackal quite occupied with the cubs, Dog hastened
to the kitchen, and, taking up his bone, stole out

of the house, and carried it to a considerable distance off. When he thought he was safe from observation, he lay down, and, placing the bone between his paws, was about to indulge his craving for marrow, when lo ! the bone was seen to fly away back to the den. Wondering at such a curious event, furious at his disappointment, and somewhat alarmed as he remembered Leopardess's warning words, he rushed after it, crying :

"Jackal, Jackal ! shut the door ; the bone is coming. Jackal, please shut the door."

Jackal fortunately was at the door, squatting on his haunches, having just arrived there from nursing the cubs, and saw the bone coming straight towards him, and Dog galloping and crying out to shut the door. Quickly perceiving that Dog had at last allowed his appetite to get the better of his duty, and having, truth to say, a fellow-feeling for his fellow-servant, Jackal closed the door just in time, for in about a second afterwards the bone struck the door with a tremendous force, dinting it deeply.

Then Jackal turned to Dog, on recovering from his astonishment, and angrily asked, "Oh, Dog, do you know what you are doing ? Have you no sense ? You came near being the death of me this time. I'll tell you what, my friend, if

Mistress Leopardess hears of this, your life is not worth a feather."

" Now don't, please, good Jackal—don't say anything of it this time. The fright I have had is quite sufficient to keep me from touching a bone again."

" Well, I am sure I don't wish you any harm, but for your life's sake do not be so dull as to forget the lesson you have learned."

Soon after Leopardess returned with a small antelope for the morrow's breakfast, and cried out to Jackal, as was usual with her on returning from the hunt :

" Now, my Jackal, bring the cubs hither ; my dugs are so heavy. How are the little ones ? "

" Ah, very well, ma'am : poor little dears, they have been in a sweet sleep ever since you went out."

A few days later, Leopardess brought a fat young zebra, and Jackal displayed his best skill in preparing it for dinner. Dog also assisted with wise suggestions in the preparation of certain auxiliaries to the feast. When all was ready, Dog laid the table, and as fast as Jackal brought the various dishes, Dog arranged them in the most tempting manner on fresh banana leaves, spread over the ample plateau. Just before sitting down to the meal, Leopardess heard a strange noise without, and bounded to the door, growling angrily at being disturbed. Dog instantly seized the opportunity of her absence to extract a great bone from one of the trays, and stowed it in a recess in a wall of the passage leading from the kitchen. Presently Leopardess came back, and when the cubs were brought the meal was proceeded with in silence. When they had all eaten enough, the good effect of it was followed by commendations upon the cooking, and the juicy flavour of the meat, and how well Jackal had prepared everything. Neither was Dog forgotten by the mistress and her young ones, and he was dismissed with the plenteous remnants of the feast for himself and mate, with the courteous hope that they would find enough and to spare.

In the afternoon Leopardess, having refreshed herself with a nap, sallied out once more, enjoining Jackal, as she was going out of the den, to be attentive to her little ones during her absence.

While his friend Jackal proceeded towards the cubs, Dog surreptitiously abstracted his bone from the cavity in the passage wall, and trotted out unobserved. When he had arrived at a secluded place, he lay down, and, seizing the bone between his paws, was about to give it a preliminary lick,

when again, to his dismay and alarm, the bone
flew up and away straight for the door. Dog
loped after it as fast as his limbs could carry him,
crying out :

"Oh, Jackal, Jackal, good Jackal ! Shut the
door. Hurry up. Shut the door, good Jackal."

Again Jackal heard his friend's cry, and sprang
up to close the door, and the instant he had done
so the bone struck it with dreadful force.

Turning to the crestfallen and panting dog,
Jackal said sternly : "You are a nice fellow, you
are. I well see the end of you. Now listen, this
is the last time that I shall help you, my friend.
The next time you take a bone you will bear the
consequences, so look out."

"Come, Jackal, now don't say any more ; I will
not look at a bone again, I make you a solemn
promise."

"Keep to that, and you will be safe," replied
Jackal.

Poor Dog, however, was by no means able to
adhere to his promise, for a few days afterwards
Leopardess brought a fat young eland, and he
found an opportunity to abstract a fine marrow-
bone before serving his generous mistress. Late in
the afternoon, after dinner and siesta, Leopardess,
before going out, repeated her usual charge to

Jackal, and while the faithful servant retired to his nursing duties, greedy Dog sought his bone, and stole out to the forest with it. This time he went further than usual. Jackal meanwhile finding the cubs indisposed for sleep, led them out to the door of the den, where they frisked and gambolled about with all the liveliness of cubhood. Jackal was sitting at a distance from the door when he heard the cries of Dog. "Oh, Jackal, Jackal, good Jackal. Shut the door quickly. Look out for the bone. It is coming. Shut the door quickly."

"Ha, ha! friend Dog! At it again, eh?" said the Jackal. "It is too late, too late, Doggie dear, the cubs are in the doorway." He looked up, however, saw the bone coming with terrific speed; he heard it whiz as it flew close over his head, and almost immediately after it struck one of the cubs, killing it instantly.

Jackal appeared to quickly realise the consequences of Dog's act, and his own carelessness, and feeling that henceforth Leopardess's den would be no home for him, he resolved to escape. Just then Dog came up, and when he saw the dead cub he set up a piteous howl.

"Aye," said Jackal. "You fool, you begin to see what your greed has brought upon us all. Howl on, my friend, but you will howl differently when Mistress Leopardess discovers her dead cub. Bethink yourself how all this will end. Our mighty mistress, if she catches you, will make mince-meat of you. Neither may I stay longer here. My home must be a burrow in the wild wood, or in the rocky cave in future. What will you do ? "

" I, Jackal ? I know not yet. Go, if you will, and starve yourself. I trust to find a better home than a cramped burrow, or the cold shelter of a cave. I love warmth, and kitchen fires, and the smell of roast meats too well to trust myself to the chilly covert you propose to seek, and my coat is too fine for rough outdoor life."

" Hark ! " cried Jackal, " do you hear that ? That is the mistress's warning note ! Fare you well, Doggie. I shall dream of you to-night lying stark under the paw of the Leopardess."

Jackal waited to say no more, but fled from the scene, and from that day to this Jackal has been a vagabond. He loves the darkness, and the twilight. It is at such times you. hear his yelp. He is very selfish and cowardly. He has not courage enough to kill anything for himself, but prefers to wait—licking his chops—until the lion or the leopard, who has struck the game, has gorged himself.

As for Dog he was sorely frightened, but after a

"DOG . . . . SET UP A PITEOUS HOWL."

little deliberation he resolved to face the matter out until he was certain of the danger. He conveyed the cubs, living and dead, quickly within, and then awaited with well-dissembled anxiety the coming of his mistress.

Leopard shortly arrived, and was met at the door by the obsequious Dog with fawning welcome.

"Where is Jackal?" asked Leopardess as she entered.

"I regret to say he has not returned yet from a visit which he said he was bound to pay his friends and family, whom he had not seen for so long," replied Dog.

"Then you go and bring my little ones to me. Poor little dears, they must be hungry by this, and my milk troubles me," commanded the mistress.

Dog departed readily, thinking to himself, "I am in for it now." He soon returned, bearing one of the cubs, and laid it down.

"Bring the other one, quickly," cried Leopardess.

"Yes, ma'am, immediately," he said.

Dog took the same cub up again, but in a brief time returned with it. The cub, already satisfied, would not touch the teat.

"Go and bring the other one, stupid," cried Leopardess, observing that it would not suck.

"This is the other one, mistress," he replied.

" Then why does it not suck ? " she asked.

" Perhaps it has not digested its dinner."

" Where is Jackal ?   Has he not yet returned ?
Jackal ! " she cried.   " Where are you, Jackal ? "

From the jungle out-doors Jackal shrilly yelped,
" Here I am, mistress ! "

" Come   to   me   this   instant," commanded
Leopardess.

" Coming, mistress, coming," responded Jackal's
voice faintly, for at the sound of her call he had
been alarmed and was trotting off.

" Why, what can be the matter with the brute,
trifling with me in this manner.   Here, Dog, take
this cub to the crib."

Dog hastened to obey, but Leopardess, whose
suspicions had been aroused, quietly followed him
as he entered the doorway leading into the inner
recess of the house where the crib was placed.
Having placed the living near the dead cub in the
crib, Dog turned to leave, when he saw his dreaded
mistress in the doorway, gazing with fierce distended eyes, and it flashed on him that she had
discovered the truth, and fear adding speed to his
limbs he darted like an arrow between her legs,
and rushed out of the den.   With a loud roar of
fury Leopardess sprang after him, Dog running for
dear life.   His mistress was gaining upon him,

when Dog turned aside, and ran round the trees. Again Leopardess was rapidly drawing near, when Dog shot straight away and increased the distance between them a little. Just as one would think Dog had no hope of escaping from his fierce mistress, he saw a wart-hog's burrow, into which he instantly dived. Leopardess arrived at the hole in the ground as the tail of Dog disappeared from her sight. Being too large of body to enter, she tore up the entrance to the burrow, now and then extending her paw far within to feel for her victim. But the burrow was of great length, and ran deep downwards, and she was at last obliged to desist from her frantic attempts to reach the runaway.

Reflecting awhile, Leopardess looked around and saw Monkey near by, sitting gravely on a branch watching her.

"Come down, Monkey," she imperatively commanded, "and sit by this burrow and watch the murdering slave who is within, while I procure materials to smoke him out."

Monkey obeyed, and descending the tree, took his position at the mouth of the burrow. But it struck him that should Dog venture out, his strength would be unable to resist him. He therefore begged Leopardess to stay a moment, while he went to bring a rock with which he could block the hole securely. When this was done, Leopardess said, "Now stay here, and do not stir until I return ; I will not be long, and when I come I will fix him."

Leopardess, leaving the burrow in charge of Monkey, commenced to collect a large quantity of dry grass, and then proceeded to her house to procure fire wherewith to light it, and suffocate Dog with the smoke.

Dog, soon after entering the burrow had turned himself round and faced the hole, to be ready for all emergencies. He had heard Leopardess give her orders to Monkey, had heard Monkey's plans for blockading him, as well as the threat of Leopardess to smoke him out. There was not much hope for him if he stayed longer.

After a little while he crept close to the rock that blocked his exit, and whispered :

"Monkey, let me out, there's a good fellow."

"It may not be," replied Monkey.

"Ah, Monkey, why are you so cruel ? I have not done any harm to you. Why do you stand guard over me to prevent my escape ? "

"I am simply obeying orders, Dog. Leopardess said, 'Stay here and watch, and see that Dog does not escape ;' and I must do so or harm will come to me, as you know."

Then said Dog, "Monkey, I see that you have a cruel heart, too, though I thought none but the Leopard kind could boast of that. May you feel some day the deep despair I feel in my heart. Let me say one word more to you before I die. Put your head close to me that you may hear it."

Monkey, curious to know what the last word could be about, put his face close between the rock

"DOG FLED LIKE THE WIND."

and the earth and looked in, upon which Dog threw so much dust and sand into his cunning eyes as almost to blind him.

Monkey staggered back from the entrance, and while knuckling his eyes to rub the sand out, Dog put his fore-feet against the rock and soon rolled it away. Then, after a hasty view around, Dog fled like the wind from the dangerous spot.

Monkey, after clearing his eyes from the dust

thrown in them, and reviewing his position, began to be concerned as to his own fate. It was not long before his crafty mind conceived that it would be a good idea to place some soft nuts within the burrow, and roll back the stone into its place.

When Leopardess returned with the fire she was told that Dog was securely imprisoned within, upon which she piled the grass over the burrow and set fire to it.

Presently a cracking sound was heard within.

"What can that be?" demanded Leopardess.

"That must surely be one of Dog's ears that you heard exploding," replied Monkey.

After a short time another crackling sound was heard.

"And what is that?" asked Leopardess.

"Ah, that must be the other ear of course," Monkey answered.

But as the fire grew hotter and the heat increased within there were a great many of these sounds heard, at which Monkey laughed gleefully and cried:

"Ah ha! do you hear? Dog is splitting to pieces now. Oh, he is burning up finely; every bone in his body is cracking. Ah, but it is a cruel death, though, is it not?"

"Let him die," fiercely cried Leopardess. "He

killed one of my young cubs—one of the loveliest little fellows you ever saw."

Both Leopardess and Monkey remained at the burrow until the fire had completely died out, then the first said :

" Now, Monkey, bring me a long stick with a hook at the end of it, that I may rake Dog's bones out and feast my eyes upon them."

Monkey hastened to procure the stick, with which the embers were raked out, when Leopardess exclaimed :

" What a queer smell this is ! It is not at all like what one would expect from a burnt dog."

" Ah," replied Monkey, " Dog must be completely burnt by this. Of that there can be no doubt. Did you ever burn a dog before that you know the smell of its burnt body so well ? "

" No," said the Leopardess ; " but this is not like the smell of roast meat. Rake out all the ashes that I may see the bones and satisfy myself."

Monkey, compelled to do as he was commanded, put in his stick, and drew out several half-baked nuts, the shells of which were cracked and gaping open. These Leopardess no sooner saw than she seized Monkey, and furiously cried :

" You wretch, you have deceived and trifled with me ! You have permitted the murderer of my cub to escape, and your life shall now be the forfeit for his."

" Pardon, mighty Leopardess, but let me ask how do you propose to slay me ? "

" Why, miserable slave, how else should I kill you but with one scratch of my claws ? "

" Nay, then, great Queen, my blood will fall on your head and smother you. It is better for yourself that you should toss me up above that thorny bough, so that when I fall upon it the thorns may penetrate my heart and kill me."

No sooner had Monkey ended, than fierce Leopardess tossed Monkey upward as he had directed ; but the latter seized the bough and sat up, and from this he sprang upward into another still higher, and thence from branch to branch and from tree to tree until he was safe from all possible pursuit.

Leopardess perceived that another of her intended victims had escaped, and was furious with rage.

" Come down this instant," she cried to Monkey, hoping he would obey her.

" Nay, Leopardess. It has been told me, and the forest is full of the report, that your cruelty has driven from you Jackal and Dog, and that they will never serve you again. Cruel people never can reckon upon friends. I and my tribe, so long servants to you, will henceforth be strangers to you. Fare you well."

A great rustling was heard in the trees overhead as Monkey and his tribe migrated away from the district of the cruel Leopardess who, devoured with rage, was obliged to depart with not one of her vengeful thoughts.gratified.

As she was returning to her den, Leopardess bethought herself of the Oracle, who was her friend, who would no doubt, at her solicitations, reveal the hiding-places of Jackal and Dog. She directed her steps to the cave of the Oracle, who was a nondescript practising witchcraft in the wildest part of the district.

To this curious being she related the story of the murder of her cub by Jackal and Dog, and requested him to inform her by what means she could discover the criminals and wreak her vengeance on them.

The Oracle replied, " Jackal has gone into the wild wood, and he and his family henceforward will always remain there, to degenerate in time into a suspicious and cowardly race. Dog has fled to take his shelter in the home of man, to be his companion and friend, and to serve man against you and your kind. But lest you accuse me of ill-will to you, I will tell you how you may catch Dog if you are clever and do not allow your temper to exceed your caution. Not far off is a village belonging to one of the human tribes, near which there is a large ant-hill, where moths every morning flit about in the sunshine of the early day. About the same time Dog leaves the village to sport and gambol and chase the moths. If you can find a lurking-place not far from it, where you can lie silently in wait, Dog may be caught by you in an unwary moment while at his daily play. I have spoken."

Leopardess thanked the Oracle and retired brooding over its advice. That night the moon was very clear and shining bright, and she stole out of her den, and proceeding due west as she was directed, in a few hours she discovered the village and the ant-hill described by the Oracle. Near the mound she also found a thick dense bush, which was made still more dense by the tall wild grass surrounding it. In the depths of this she crouched, waiting for morning. At dawn the village wherein men and women lived was astir, and at sunrise the gates were opened. A little later Dog signalled himself by his well-known barks as he came out to take his morning's exercise. Unsuspicious of the presence of his late dread mistress he bounded up the hill and began to circle around, chasing the lively moths. Leopardess, urged by her anger, did not wait until Dog, tired with his sport, would of his own accord stray among the bushes, but uttering a loud roar sprang out from her hiding-place. Dog, warned by her voice, which he

" CAME POURING FROM THEIR HOUSES WITH DREADFUL WEAPONS."

well knew, put his tail between his legs and rushed through the open gates and alarmed his new masters, who came pouring from their houses with dreadful weapons in their hands, who chased her, and would have slain her had she not bounded over the fence. Thus Leopardess lost her last chance of revenging the death of her cub; but as she was creeping homeward her mortification was so great that she vowed to teach her young eternal hostility towards Dog and all his tribe. Dog also, convinced that his late mistress was one who nourished an implacable resentment when offended, became more cautious, and a continued life with his new masters increased his attachment for them. When he finally married, and was blessed with a progeny, he taught his pups various arts by which they might ingratiate themselves more and more with the human race. He lived in comfort and affluence to a good old age, and had the satisfaction to see his family grow more and more in the estimation of their generous masters, until dogs and men became inseparable companions.

Leopardess and her cubs removed far away from the house associated with her misfortune, but though Time healed the keen sore of her bereavement by blessing her annually with more cubs, her hate for Dog and his kind was lasting and continues to this day. And thus it was that the friendly fellowship which reigned between the forest animals during the golden age of Uganda was broken for ever.

For proof of the truth of what I have said consider the matter in your own minds. Regard the

Ape who, upon the least alarm springs up the tree, and stays not until he has secured himself far from reach.   Think of the Jackal in his cheerless solitude deep in the bowels of the earth, or in the farthest rocky recess that he can discover, ever on the watch against some foe, too full of distrust to have a friend, the most selfish and cowardly of the forest community.   The Leopard is the enemy at all times, night and day, of every animal, unless it be the lion and the elephant.   As for the Dog, where is the man who is not acquainted with his fidelity, his courage in time of danger, his watchful care of his interests by night, and his honest love for the family which feeds him.   My story is here ended.

A SECOND VERSION OF THE LEOPARD AND THE DOG STORY.

ARBOKO, who was originally from Unyoro, a country which lies to the north of Uganda, and had been employed as a page by Mtesa, king of Uganda, protested that his version of how the dog became estranged from the leopard, his chum, was nearer the truth than that given by Kadu. Perceiving that he was inclined to contribute to our amusement, for a reason of his own, we ranged ourselves around the camp fire in the usual way and prepared to listen to another version of a legend which is popular among most of the tribes dwelling in the Lake Region.

How the Dog outwitted the Leopard.*

In the early time there was a dog and a leopard dwelling together in a cave like chums. They shared and fared alike. Exact half of everything and equal effort were the terms upon which they lived. Many and many a famous raid among the flocks and fowls in the human villages they made. The leopard was by far the strongest and boldest, and was most successful in catching prey. Dog lived so well on the spoils brought home by his friend that he became at last fat and lazy, and he began to dislike going out at night in the rain and cold dew, and to hide this growing habit from Leopard he had to be very cunning. He always invented some excuse or another to explain why he brought nothing to the common larder, and finally he hit upon a new plan of saving himself from the toil and danger.

Just before dusk one day, Leopard and Dog were sociably chatting together, when Leopard said that he intended that night to catch a fine fat black goat which he had observed in the nearest village to their den. He had watched him getting

* Republished from the " Fortnightly Magazine " with the permission of the Editor and Proprietors.

fatter every day, and he was bent upon bringing him home.

" Black is it ? " cried Dog. " That is strange, for that is also the colour of the one I purposed to catch to-night."

The two friends slept until most of the night was gone, but when there were signs that morning was not far off they silently loped away to their work.

They parted at the village which Leopard had selected to rob, Dog whispering " Good luck " to him. Dog trotted off a little way and sneaked back to watch his friend.

Leopard stealthily surveying the tall fence, saw one place which he could leap over, and at one spring was inside the village. Snuffing about, he discovered the goat-pen, forced an entrance, and seizing his prize by the neck, drew it out. He then flung it over his shoulders, and with a mighty leap landed outside the fence.

Dog, who had watched his chance, now cried out in an affected voice, " Hi, hi—wake up ! Leopard has killed the goat. There he is. Ah, ah ! Kill him, kill him ! "

Alarmed at the noise made, and hearing a rustle in the grass near him, Leopard was obliged to abandon his prize, and to save his own life, dropped the goat and fled.

"LEOPARD SAW ONE PLACE WHICH HE COULD LEAP OVER."

Dog, chuckling loudly at the success of his ruse, picked the dead goat up, and trotted home to the den with it.

" Oh, see, Leopard ! " cried he, as he reached the entrance, " what a fat goat I've got at my village. Is it not a heavy one ?   But where is yours ?   Did you not succeed after all ? "

" Oh ! I was alarmed by the owners in the village, who pursued me and yelled out, ' Kill him, kill him ! ' and there was something rustling in the grass close by, and I thought that I was done for ; but I dropped the goat and ran away.   I dare say they have found the animal by this, and have eaten our meat.   Never mind, though, better luck next time.   I saw a fine fat white goat in the pen, which I am sure to catch to-morrow night."

" Well, I am very sorry, but cheer your heart. You shall have an equal share with me of this. Let us bestir ourselves to cook it."

They gathered sticks and made a fire, and began to roast it.   When it was nearly ready Dog went outside, and took a stick and beat the ground, and whined out :

" Oh ! please, I did not do it.   It was Leopard that killed the goat.   Oh ! don't kill me.   It was Leopard who stole it."

Leopard, hearing these cries and the blows of

the stick, thought to himself : " Ah ! the men have
followed us to our den, and are killing Dog ; then
they will come and kill me if I do not run." He
therefore ran out and escaped.

Dog, on seeing him well away, coolly returned
to the den and devoured the whole of the meat,
leaving only the bones.

After a long time Leopard returned to the den,
and found Dog groaning piteously. " What is the
matter, my friend ? " he asked.

" Ah ! oh ! don't touch me ; don't touch me, I
beg of you. I am so bruised and sore all over !
Ah ! my bones ! They have half killed me,"
moaned Dog.

" Poor fellow ! Well, lie still and rest. There
is nothing like rest for a bruised body. I will get
that white goat the next time I try."

After waiting two or three days, Leopard
departed to obtain the white goat. Dog sneaked
after him, and served his friend in the same way,
bringing the white goat himself, and bragging how
he had succeeded, while pretending to pity Leopard
for his bad luck.

Three times running Dog served him with the
same trick, and Leopard was much mortified at
his own failure. Then Leopard thought of the
Muzimu—the oracle who knows all things, and

gives such good advice to those who are unfortunate and ask for his help—and he resolved, in his distress, to seek him.

In the heart of the tall, dark woods, where the bush is most dense, where vines clamber over the clumps, and fold themselves round and round the trees, and hang in long coils by the side of a cool stream, the Muzimu resided.

Leopard softly drew near the sacred place and cried, " Oh ! Muzimu, have pity on me. I am almost dying with hunger. I used to be bold and strong, and successful, but now, of late, though I catch my prey as of old, something always happens to scare me away, and I lose the meat I have taken. Help me, oh ! Muzimu, and tell me how my good luck may return."

After a while the Muzimu answered in a deep voice, " Leopard, your ill-luck comes from your own folly. You know how to catch prey, but it takes a dog to know how to eat it. Go ; watch your friend, and your ill-luck will fly away."

Leopard was never very wise, though he had good eyes, and was swift and brave, and he thought over what the Muzimu said. He could not understand in what way his good luck would return by watching his friend, but he resolved to follow the advice of the Muzimu.

The next night Leopard gave out that he was
going to seize a dun-coloured goat, and Dog said,
"Ah! that is what I mean to do too. I think
a dun-coated goat so sweet."

The village was reached, a low place was found
in the palings, and Leopard, as quick as you could
wink, was over and among the goats. With one
stroke he struck his victim dead, threw it over his
shoulders, and, with a flying leap, carried it outside. Dog, who was hiding near the place, in a
strange voice cried, "Ah! here he is—the thief of
a Leopard! Kill him! kill him!"

Leopard turning his head around, saw him in
the grass and heard him yelp, "Awu-ou-ou!
Awu-ou-ou! Kill him! kill him!" dropped the
goat for an instant and said, "Ah, it is you, my
false friend, is it. Wait a bit, and I will teach
you how you may steal once too often." With eyes
like balls of fire, he rushed at him, and would have
torn him in pieces, but Dog's instinct told him that
the game he had been playing was up, and bury-
ing his tail between his hind legs, he turned and
fled for dear life. Round and round the village he
ran, darting this way and that, until, finding his
strength was oozing out of him, he dashed finally
through a gap in the fence, straight into a man's
house and under the bed, where he lay gasping

and panting.　Seeing that the man, who had been
scared by his sudden entry, was about to take his
spear to kill him, he crawled from under the bed
to the man's feet, and licked them, and turned on
his back imploring mercy.　The man took pity on
him, tied him up, and made a pet of him.　Ever
since Dog and Man have been firm friends, but
a mortal hatred has existed between Dog and
Leopard.　Dog's back always bristles straight up
when his enemy is about, and there is no truer
warning of the Leopard's presence than that given
by Dog—while Leopard would rather eat a dog
than a goat any day.　That is the way—as I
heard it in Unyoro—that the chumship between
Leopard and Dog was broken up.

THE LEGEND OF THE CUNNING TERRAPIN
AND THE CRANE.

THE following story of the cunning Terrapin and the Crane established Kadu's reputation among us, and the Zanzibaris were never so amused as on this evening.

"Master," began Kadu, after we had made ourselves comfortable before a bright and crackling fire, "some men say that animals do not reason, and cannot express themselves, but I should like to know how it is that we perceive that there is great cunning in their actions, as though they calculated beforehand how to act, and what would be the result. We Waganda think animals are very clever. We observe the cock in the yard, and the hen with her chickens; the leopard, as he is about to pounce on his prey; the lion, as he is about to attack; the crocodile, as he prepares for his rush;

the buffalo in the shade, as he awaits the hunter ; the elephant, as he stands at attention ; and we say to ourselves, how intelligent they are ! Our legends are all founded on these things, and we interpret the actions of animals from having seen their methods ; and I think men placed in the same circumstances could not have acted much better. It may appear to you, as though we were telling you mere idle tales to raise a laugh. Well, it may be very amusing to hear and talk about them, but it is still more amusing to watch the tricks of animals and insects, and our old men are fond of quoting the actions of animals to teach us, while we are children, what we ought to do. Indeed, there is scarcely a saying but what is founded upon something that an animal was seen to do at one time or another.

" Now the story that I am about to relate, is a very old one in Uganda. I heard it when a child, and from a fact that a Terrapin was said to be so cunning, I have never liked to ill-treat a Terrapin, and every time I see one, the story comes to my mind in all its freshness."

A Terrapin and a Crane were one time travelling together very sociably. They began their conversation by the Terrapin asking :

" How is your family to-day, Miss Crane ? "

" Oh, very well. Mamma, who is getting old, complains now and then, that's all."

" But do you know that it strikes me that she is very fat ? " said Terrapin. " Now a thought has just entered my head, which I beg to propose to you. My mother, too, is ailing, and I am rather tired of hearing her complaints day after day ; but she is exceedingly lean and tough, though there is plenty of her. I wonder what you will say to my plan ? We are both hungry. So let us go and kill your mother, and eat her ; and to-morrow, you will come to me, and we will kill my mother. We thus shall be supplied with meat for some days."

Replied the Crane, " I like the idea greatly, and agree to it. Let us go about it at once, for hunger is an exacting mistress, and the days of fasting are more frequent than those of fulness."

The matricides turned upon their tracks, and, arriving at the house of Mrs. Crane, the two cruel creatures seized upon Mamma Crane, and put her to death. They then plucked her clean, and placed her body in the stew-pot, and both Terrapin and Crane feasted.

Terrapin then crawled home, leaving Crane to sleep, and the process of digestion. But, alas ! Crane became soon very ill. Whether some qualms of conscience disturbed digestion or not, I cannot say, but she passed a troublesome night, and for several days afterwards she did not stir from her house.

Terrapin, on reaching the house of its mamma, which was in the hollow of a tree, cried out :

" Tu-no-no-no !" upon which Mrs. Terrapin said, " Oh, that is my child," and she let down a cord, to which young Terrapin made himself fast, and was assisted to the nest where the parent had already prepared a nice supper for him.

Several days later, Terrapin was proceeding through the woods to the pool where he was accustomed to bathe, when at the water-side he met Miss Crane apparently quite spruce and strong again.

She hailed Terrapin and said, " Oh, here you are, at last. I have been waiting to see you for some time."

" Yes," replied Terrapin, " here I am, and you —how do you feel now ? My neighbours told me you were very ill."

" I am all right again," said Miss Crane, " but I think my old ma disagreed with me, and I was quite poorly for some days ; but I am now anxious to know when you are going to keep your part of the bargain which we made ? "

" What—you mean about the disposing of my old ma ? "

" Yes, to be sure," answered Crane, " I feel quite hungry."

" Well, well. Bargains should always be kept, for if the blood-oath be broken misfortune follows. Your mother's death rests on my head, and I mean to return your hospitality with interest, otherwise, may my shell be soon empty of its tenant. Stay here awhile and I will bring her."

So saying, Terrapin departed, and crept to where he had secretly stowed a quantity of india-rubber, in readiness for the occasion. After taking out quite a mass of it, he returned to the pond, where Miss Crane stood on one leg, expectant and winking pleasantly.

" I fear, sister Crane," said Terrapin, as he laid his burden down, " that you will find my old ma tough. She turned out to be much leaner than I anticipated. There is no more fat on her bones than there is on my back. But now, fall to, and welcome. There is plenty there. I am not hungry myself, as I have just finished my dinner."

Miss Crane, with her empty stomach, was not fastidious, and stepped out eagerly to the feast so faithfully provided, and began to tear away at what Terrapin had brought. The rubber, however, stretched by the greedy crane, suddenly flew from her foot, and rebounding, struck her in the face a smart blow.

"Oh ! oh !" cried Crane, confused with the blow. "Your old ma is most tough."

"Yes, she is. I suspected she would prove a little tough," answered Terrapin, with a chuckle. "But don't be bashful. Eat away, and welcome."

Again Miss Crane tugged at the rubber to tear it, but the more it was stretched, the more severe were the shocks she received, and her left eye was almost blinded.

"Well, I never," exclaimed Miss Crane. "She is too tough altogether."

"Try again," cried Terrapin. "Try again ; little by little, it is said, a fly eats a cow's tail. You will get a rare and tender bit in time."

Miss Crane thus pressed, did so, and seizing a piece lay back, and drew on it so hard that when the rubber at last slipped, it bounded back with such force, that she was sent sprawling to the ground.

"Why, what is the matter ?" asked Terrapin, pretending to be astonished. "She is tough, I admit ; but loh ! our family are famous for toughness. However, the tougher it is, the longer it lasts on the stomach. Try again, sister Crane ; I warrant you will manage it next time."

" Oh, bother your old ma. Eat her yourself. I have had enough of that kind of meat."

" You give it up, do you ? " cried Terrapin. " Well, well, it is a pity to throw good meat away. Maybe, if I keep it longer it will get tenderer by and by."

They thus parted. Terrapin bearing his share of rubber away in one direction, and Miss Crane sadly disgusted, striding grandly off in another, but looking keenly about for something to satisfy her hunger.

When she had gone a great distance, a parrot flew across her path, and perching on a branch near her, cried out, " Oh, royal bird, say since when has rubber become the food of the bird-king's family ? "

" What do you mean, Parrot ? " she asked.

" Well, I saw you tearing at a piece of rubber just now, and when you marched off Terrapin carried it away, and I heard him say—because he has a habit of speaking his thoughts aloud—' Oh, how stupid my sister Crane is ! She thinks my ma is dead. Ho, ho, ho ! what a stupid ! ' And all the way he chuckled and laughed as though he was filled with plantain wine."

" Is his ma not dead then ? " asked Miss Crane.

" Dead ! Not a bit of it," replied Parrot. " I saw

old Ma Terrapin but a moment ago as I flew by her tree, waiting for her son, and the cord is ready for his cry of ' Tu-no-no-no. Ano-no-no. We-no-no-no ! ' "

" Ah, Parrot, your words are good. When we know what another is saying behind our backs, we discover the workings of his heart. The words of Terrapin are like the bush that covers the trap. Good-bye Parrot. When we next meet, we shall have another story to tell."

On the next day, Terrapin observed Miss Crane approaching his house, and he advanced a little way to meet her.

" Well, sister Crane, I hope you are all right this morning ? " he asked.

" Oh, yes, so so, brother Terrapin. But you must excuse me just now ; I've heard bad news from my family. A brother and sister of mine are suddenly taken ill, and I am bound to go and visit them," answered Crane.

"Ah, Miss Crane, that reminds me of my own brother and sister, who are much younger than I am, but very soft and tender. What do you say now to making another bargain ? " asked Terrapin with a wink.

" You are very good, Terrapin. I will think of it as I go along. I shall be back before noon to-

morrow, and we will talk of a trade then." They
were very civil to one another as they parted.
Terrapin went for his usual walk to the pond, Miss
Crane proceeded to visit her family, but muttered :

"Ha, ha, Terrapin, you are great at a trade ;
but you will not make another with me in a hurry
till our first one is squared."

After she had gone a little way she turned
suddenly round and came back to the foot of
Terrapin's tree, and cried,

"Tu-no-no-no. Ano-no-no-no. We-no-no-no !"

" Ah, that is my child's voice," said Ma Terrapin
to herself, and let down the cord.

Miss Crane caught hold and climbed up towards
the nest. Ma Terrapin craned her neck out far to
welcome her child, but before she could discover
by what means little Terrapin had changed its
dress, Miss Crane struck Ma Terrapin with her
long sharp bill in the place where the neck joins
the shoulder, and in a short time Ma Terrapin was
as dead as Miss Crane's own mother.

The body was rolled from the nest, and it
went falling down, and Miss Crane slid quickly
after it.

In a quiet place screened by thick bushes Miss
Crane made a great fire, with which Ma Terrapin's
thick shell was cracked. She then scooped out the

flesh, and carried it to her own home, and stowed it in a big black pot.

On the next day as Miss Crane was standing on one leg by the pond, with her head half buried in her feathers, who should come along but Terrapin, crying bitterly, and saying, " Ah, my ma is dead. My old ma has been killed. Who will assist me now ? "

Miss Crane affected to be asleep, but heard every word. When, however, Terrapin was near, she woke up suddenly and said, cheerfully :

" Ah ! it is Terrapin, my little brother Terrapin. How do you do to-day ? "

Now as Terrapin had already slain his mother, according to his own confession, it struck him that it would not do to accuse Miss Crane of the murder, because by doing so he would expose his breach of faith with her, but the scent of the roasted flesh of Ma Terrapin came strong just then, and he knew that it was Crane who, discovering his trick, had killed her.

He managed, however, to reply briskly :

" Sissy, dear, I am but tolerable. But how is your family to-day ? "

" My brother and sister are much improved, Terrapin. They are both as fat as tallow. By-the-bye, what about that trade you proposed to me ? "

"I am ready, Miss Crane for a trade any day. When shall it be?"

"No time so good as the present, and if you jog along to the other end of the pond, I will fix my house here, and soon catch up with you."

Terrapin professed great delight, and toddled along; but when he had gone a little way his bad habit of thinking aloud came on him, and he was heard to say:—

"My poor ma! my poor ma is dead! Oh you wicked Crane. I know by the scent of the meat that you have killed my ma. What can I do now?"

Miss Crane knew then that she had been discovered, and she began to think that it was time to remove to another district, for Terrapin had many friends in the woods, such as rabbits, jackals, lions, and serpents, and if Terrapin moaned so loud, all the people of the woods would know what she had done, and many would no doubt assist him to punish her. Casting about in her mind for the best place, she remembered an extremely tall tree which was not far from Terrapin's house, a very lofty clean-shafted tree, on the top of which she would be safe from surprise.

Thither she hastily removed her belongings, and soon established herself comfortably. She had also provided herself with a store of strong sticks to be used as weapons in case of necessity.

Terrapin meanwhile crawled along, moaning loudly his lamentations. Suddenly Rabbit popped out of the woods, and stood in his path. He soon was made aware of Terrapin's bereavement, and strongly sympathised with him. Terrapin related the story in such a way that made Miss Crane appear to be a murderess, against whom the people of the woods should take vengeance.

"Then," said Rabbit, "that must be Miss Crane, who is building her house on the very top of that tall tree near your place."

"Is she?" asked Terrapin. "I did not know that. She was to have met me here; but I see she knows that she is detected, and is already taking measures to protect herself. But, Rabbit, you who are always wise, tell me how I may avenge myself?"

"There is only one way that I know of," answered Rabbit, dubiously. "Go to the Soko (Gorilla?), but he is a hard dealer who will make you pay handsomely for his help. Soko is the king of the ape kind. If you pay him well, he will fasten a cord to Crane's nest, up which you can climb when she is absent. Once there, lie quietly, and when she alights seize her."

The plan pleased Terrapin immensely, and possessing a comfortable property upon the loss of his mother, he thought he had sufficient to purchase Soko's assistance.

Through the good offices of Rabbit negotiations were entered into with Soko, who agreed for a potful of good nuts, ten bunches of ripe bananas, one hundred eggs, and sundry other trifles, to hang a stout rattan climber to Crane's nest, long enough to reach the ground.

The royal bird was soon informed of the conspiracy against her by the Parrot, who loves to carry tales, and Miss Crane resolved to be absent from home while Soko was fastening the climber, but commissioned her friend the Parrot to observe the proceedings, and to report to her when Soko had completed his task.

Soko performed his part expeditiously. Terrapin tested the strength of the rattan, and had to confess that Soko had earned his pay, and Rabbit accompanied Terrapin and Soko to Terrapin's house to see the Soko receive his commission.

As they departed Parrot flew to inform Miss Crane, who immediately returned to her house to await her enemy.

Not long after Terrapin came to the foot of Crane's tree and commenced to climb up. He had

"SOKO PERFORMED HIS PART EXPEDITIOUSLY."

nearly reached the top when Miss Crane stood up and delivered such a thwacking blow on Terrapin's back that caused him to loose his hold and fall to the ground. When Terrapin recovered his senses, he heard Miss Crane cry out—

"Ha ! brother Terrapin, that was a nasty fall. You remember the rubber, don't you ? There is nothing like the advice you gave me. Try again, Terrapin, my brother. Try again."

"You killed my ma, did you not ? " asked Terrapin.

" I thought you told me that you had killed her according to agreement. Then how can you say that I killed her ? " asked Miss Crane.

"That was not my ma I gave you. It was only a lump of rubber."

" Ho, ho ! You confess it then ? Well, we are now quits. You induced me to kill my ma, and as you could not keep your part of the bargain, I saved you the trouble. My ma was as much to me as your ma was to you. We have both lost our ma's now. So let us call it even, and be friends again."

Terrapin hesitated, but the memory of his ma's loss soon produced the old bitterness, and he became as unforgiving as ever. Miss Crane must, however, be persuaded that the matter was forgiven, otherwise he would never have the opportunity to revenge his ma's death.

"All right, Crane," he answered; "but let me come up, and embrace you over it, or do you descend and let us shake hands."

"Come up, by all means, Terrapin. I am always at home to friends," said Miss Crane.

Terrapin upon this began to climb, but as he was ascending he foolishly began to think aloud again, and he was heard saying—

"Oh, yes, sister Crane. Just wait a little, and you will see. He, he, he!"

Miss Crane, who was quietly listening, heard Terrapin's chuckle and muttering, and prepared to receive him properly. When he was within reach, she cried, "Hold hard, Terrapin," and at once proceeded to shower mighty blows on his back, then laid the stick on his feet so sharply that, to protect them, he had to withdraw them into his shell, in doing which he lost his hold and fell to the ground with such force that to anything but a terrapin the great fall would have been instantly fatal.

"Try again, Terrapin; try again, my brother. Another time and you will succeed," cried Miss Crane, mockingly.

Terrapin slowly recovered his faculties from the

"HOLD HARD, TERRAPIN!"

second fall, and exclaimed, " Ah, Crane, Crane. If I heed you a second time, call me fool. Yesterday and to-day you triumphed, to-morrow will be my turn."

" *Kwa-le, kwa-le,*" Miss Crane shrilly cried. " My tree will stand to-morrow where it stood to-day. You know the way to it; if not, your hate will find it."

Terrapin toddled away upon this to seek the lion, to whom, when he had found him, he pleaded so powerfully that the Lion pitied him greatly, and answered, " I may not help you in this matter, for I was not made to climb trees. Go you, and tell Jackal your story, and he will be able to advise you."

Acting on the friendly advice, Terrapin sought out the Jackal, to whom he repeated his lamentable tale. The Jackal rewarded him with a sympathetic sigh, and said, " Friend Terrapin, my teeth are sharp and my feet are swift, but, though I am so happily endowed, I have no wings to fly. Go and seek Elephant. His strength is so great that perhaps he will be able to pull the tree down for you."

Terrapin proceeded on his way to search out the Elephant, and, after much patient travel, discovered him brooding under a thick shade. To him at once

Terrapin unburdened his breast of its load of grief, and appealed piteously for his assistance.

" Little Terrapin," replied the kindly Elephant, " your tale is dour. But though I am strong, there are some things that I cannot do. Miss Crane's house is built on one of the biggest trees of the forest, and it would require two score of elephants to drag it down. It is wisdom, and not strength, that you need. Go you and seek Serpent, and he will assist you."

Thence Terrapin went to seek Serpent, and, after long seeking, found him coiled, in many shining folds, in the fork of a sturdy tree.

" Ah, Serpent," he cried, " you are a kinsman of mine, and I have long sought you. I am in dire distress, my friend," and he proceeded to inveigh against Miss Crane passionately, and concluded by invoking his assistance.

" Help me this day," cried Terrapin, " and you shall be my father and my mother, and all my nearest relations in one."

" It is well," replied the Serpent, in his slow, deliberate manner. " Miss Crane shall die, and here I make a pact with you. There shall be no enmity for all future time between your family and mine. Go now, and rest in peace, for the fate of Crane is fixed."

In the darkness of the night Serpent roused himself from his sleep and, uncoiling himself, descended the tree and glided noiselessly along the

" POOR MISS CRANE WAS FAST ASLEEP."

ground towards Miss Crane's tree. The tall clean shaft could not arrest those spiring movements, and the Serpent steadily ascended until he gained the fork. Thence, by an almost imperceptible motion, he advanced towards the nest. Poor Miss Crane was fast asleep, dreaming of the fall of Terrapin, while the Serpent folded his extremity around a stout branch and stood up prepared to strike. Quick as one could wink the Serpent flung himself upon the bird-queen, and in a moment she lay crushed and mangled. Then, seizing her body with his jaws, the Serpent slid down the shaft of the tree and sought Terrapin's house, and laid her remains before him. Terrapin was overjoyed, and invited Serpent to share with him the dainty feast which the body of Miss Crane supplied.

From that day to this Serpent and Terrapin have remained close friends, and neither have ever been known to break the solemn agreement that was made between them on the day that Terrapin solicited the help of Serpent against the bird-queen.

THE LEGEND OF KIBATTI THE LITTLE, WHO CONQUERED ALL THE GREAT ANIMALS.

HAVE done my very best to translate this story as closely as possible in order to give the faithful sense of what was said, yet I despair of rendering the little touches and flourishes which Kadu knew so well how to give with voice, gesture, and mobile face.

"Friends and freemen," he said, when we were all in listening attitude, " if a son of man knows how to show anger, I need not tell you who are experienced in travel and in the nature of beasts, that the animals of the wilds also know how to

show their spite and their passions." The legend
of Kibatti runs upon this.

On a day ages ago the great animals of the
world, consisting of the elephant, the rhinoceros,
the buffalo, the lion, the leopard, and hyena,
assembled in council in the midst of a forest not
far from a village on the frontier of Uganda. The
elephant being acknowledged by general consent as
the strongest, presided on the occasion.

Waving his trunk, and trumpeting to enjoin
silence, he said : " Friends, we are gathered together
to-day to consider how we may repay in some
measure the injuries daily done to us and our kin
by the sons of men. Not far from here is situated
a village, whence the vicious two-footed animals
issue out to make war upon all of us, who possess
double the number of feet they have. Without
warning of hostility or publishing of cause, they
deliberately leave their conical nests, day by day,
with fellest intent against any of us whom they
may happen to meet during the shining of the sun.
Wherefore we are met upon common grounds to
devise how we may retaliate upon them the wanton
outrages they daily perpetrate upon our unfortunate
kind. Personally, I have many injuries to the
elephants of my tribe to remember, and which I am
not likely to forget. It was only a week ago that

a promising child of my sister fell into a deep pit,
and was impaled on a sharp stake set in the bottom
of it; and but a few days before my youngest
brother fell head-foremost into a horribly deep
excavation that was dug, and which was artfully
concealed by leaves and grass, whereby none but
those, like myself, experienced in their guileful
arts, could have escaped. Ye have all, I daresay,
been similarly persecuted, and have deep injuries
to revenge. I wait to hear what ye propose.
Brother Rhinoceros, thou art the next to me in
bigness and strength, speak."

" Well, brother Elephant and friends, the words
we have heard are true. The son of man is, of all
creatures that I know, the most wanton in offence
against us of the four-footed tribes. Not a day
passes but I hear moan and plaint from some
sufferer. Not long ago, a cousin, walking quietly
through a wood not far from here, caught his foot
in a vine that lay across the path, and almost
immediately after a hardened and pointed stake
was precipitated from above deep into the jointure
of the neck with the spine, which killed him
instantly, of course. I have, by wonderful good
luck, escaped thus far, but it may be my fate to fall
to-morrow through some foul practice. Wherefore,
I think it were well that we set about doing what

we decide to do instanter. I propose that early in the morning, before a glint of sunshine be seen, we set upon the piratical nest and utterly destroy it. I am so loaded with hate of them, that I could dispose of the half of the rascals myself, before they could recover their wits. But if any of ye here has a better plan, I lend my ears to the hearing of it, my heart to the approval of it, and my strength and fury to the doing of it, without further speech. I have spoken."

"Now, friend Lion," said the Elephant, turning solemnly to him, "it is thy turn, and say freely what thy wit conceives in this matter. Thy courage we all know, and none of us doubt that thy mind is equal to it."

"Truly, friend Elephant, and ye others, the business we are met to consider is pressing. The sons of men are crafty, and their guile is beyond measure. The four-footed tribes have much cause of grievance against me and mine. However, none can accuse me or my family of having taken undue advantage of those whom we meditate striking. We always give loud warning, as you all know, and afterwards strike ; for if we did not do this, few of even the strongest would escape our vengeance. But these pestilent two-footed beasts—by net, trap, falling stake, pit, or noose—are unceasing in their secret malice, and there is no safety in the plain, bush, or rock-fastness against their wiles. For what I and my kin do there is good motive—that of providing meat for ourselves and young ; but it passes my wit to discover what the son of man can want with all he destroys. Even our bones—as, for instance, thy long teeth, O Elephant—they carry away with them, and even mine. I have seen the younglings of mankind dangle the teeth of my sister round their necks, and my hide appears to be so precious that the king of the village wears it over his dirty black loins. Thy tribe, O Elephant, have not much cause of complaint against me, and thou, Rhinoceros, it would tax thy memory to accuse me of aught against thy family. Brother Leopard will hold me and mine guiltless of harm to him ; so also must my cousin Hyena. Friend Buffalo and our family have sometimes a sharp quarrel, but there is no malice in it, I swear. Whereas the son of man, friends, is the common enemy of us all—it is either our flesh, or our fur, or our hide, or our teeth that he is wanting, and his whole thought is bent upon destruction pure and simple. If ye would follow me, I would glory in leading ye even now against the community, and I give ye my word that few would escape my paw and claw. However, as our object is to destroy

all, that none may escape, I agree with my friend
Rhinoceros that night-time at its blackest is safest.
Wherefore believe me that I am so sharp set for
revenge, and I feel so hollow, that nothing but the
half of all of them will satisfy my thirst for their
blood. I have ended my say."

" Now, friend Leopard, thou hadst better follow
thy cousin, and we will feel obliged to thee for the
benefit of thy advice," said the Elephant.

Leopard gave his tail a quick twirl, and licked
his chops and spoke :

" All that ye, my friends and cousin, have said,
I heartily agree and bear witness to. The spite of
the son of man towards us is limitless. It is
remarkable, too, for its cold-bloodedness and lack
of passion. We have our own quarrels in the
woods—as ye all know—and they are sharp and
quick while they last, but there is no premeditation
or malignity in what we do to one another ; but
Man, to whom we would rather give a wide berth,
if possible, pursues each of us as if his existence
depended upon the mere slaying, though I observe
that he has abundance of fruit, which ought to
satisfy any reasonable being of the ape tribe.
Wherefore, as I have many sharp reasons for
retaliation on him for his countless offences against
me and my kin, I gladly attended this council, and

"BROTHER LEOPARD WILL HOLD ME AND MINE GUILTLESS," ETC.

I will go as far as any of ye, and further if I can,
to return some of this spite on him and his tribe.
I propose that night at its darkest is best for our
plan. While the human folk are indulging in
dreams of slaughter of us, I vote that we turn
their dreams into action against themselves. The
elephant, and rhinoceros, and buffalo are strong;
let each lead his tribe to attack, overturn, and
trample down their nests. We, with our families,
will range round and slaughter every one that
escapes them. Those are my words."

"Now, friend Buffalo, what sayest thou?" demanded the Elephant. "Thou art a staunch friend
and stout foe. We cannot but listen with respect
to such an one as thyself."

"Ah, friend Elephant, and ye chiefs of tribes,
every sentiment of hostility against the vile and
spiteful sons of man that we have expressed finds
an echo in my inwards. If wrong has been done
to any here, magnify that wrong tenfold in order
that ye may understand the intensity of the hate I
bear the remorseless destroyers of my kith and kin.
Ask me not how I would slay them, my fury is
so great that I am unfit to devise. Do ye the
devising, and give the method to me. All I can
think of now is the pleasure I shall feel when my
horns are warmed in the bodies of the base and

treacherous creatures who have murdered wife,
brother, sister, and child of mine, besides a countless
number of my kindred by lance and line, spear and
snare, sword and stake, trick and trap. I will lead
my herd into the midst of the vicious community
with a joy that only my hate can match. That is
all I have to say."

" Now, my good friend Hyena. Thou art the
only one left whose sentiments are as yet unknown.
Speak, and let us hear wisdom from thee in this
matter."

The Hyena uttered a mocking laugh, and said :
" My kind friends and cousins. The night suits me
well, for I am in my element then. I may say that
I have a large family which is always hungry. It
will be a laughing matter to them indeed to hear
of your good purpose. It has been long delayed,
this signal measure of just vengeance upon those
who have outdone in cold cruelty all that generations of the four-footed tribe of the fiercest kind
have done. Bird and beast, from the smallest to
the greatest, have fallen victims to man's lust for
destruction. True, my kind are often indebted to
man for bones and refuse, but what we have eaten
has been sorely against his good will ; and we therefore owe him no gratitude. The young of the human
community will be juicy morsels for my tribe, when

the signal is given for the attack. With all my heart I say let it be to-night. I have said my say."

The Elephant then said ; " Friends, chiefs of the most powerful tribes of the forest, let it be to-night, as ye say. Let each go and muster his forces, and let the attack be in the following manner. Half-way betwixt dawn and midnight I will lead my troop from the Uganda side. The Rhinoceros will lead his from the Katonga side. The Buffalo will range his tribe along that side facing Unyoro. Behind my troop the Hyena and his families shall follow to finish those who may be but bruised by our heavy hoofs. Let Leopard place his fellows and kin in rear of the Rhinoceros troop. Lion and his great tribe are needed in rear of Buffalo's forces, for they are apt in their fury to overlook the crafty bipeds. Our object is to make a complete job of it. The sooner we part now, the fitter each will be for the perfect consummation of his long-deferred revenge."

It was well past midnight when the four-footed forces were gathered around the doomed village, and, at the shrill trumpet-note of the King Elephant, the several chiefs led their respective troops at the charge. The elephants tore on resistlessly, trampling down the domed cages of the human folk flat and level with the ground.

The rhinoceros and his host pushed on with noses
low down, and tossed the human nests as we would
kick an empty egg-basket; the buffaloes bellowed
in unison, and, closing their eyes, threw themselves
upon the huts, and gored everything within reach
of their horns. Then the fierce carnivora, all excitement at the prospect of the bloody feast, roared,
snarled, and laughed as they tore the mangled
victims piecemeal. Ah, poor village, and poor
people! In a short time the dreaming souls
dreamed no more, but were gone past recall into
the regions where dreams are unknown—all ex-
cepting one clever boy named Kibatti, and his
parents, who survived the calamity. These
happened to live in a tiny hut close hidden by a
grove of bananas on the edge of the forest, and
Kibatti about midnight had been disturbed in his
sleep by a pressure on his stomach which woke
him, and denied him further sleep. He therefore
sat sorrowing over the red embers of his fire, when
he heard the hollow tramp of large animals, and
pricking his ears, he heard trampling in another
direction; whereupon his suspicions that something
unusual was about to happen grew on him, so that
he woke his parents, and bade them listen to the
rumbling sounds that could be heard by such
experienced hunters all around them.

" Father, come, delay not ! make mother rise at once. This night my sleep has been broken as a warning to me that mischief is brewing. Let us ascend the big tree near by and observe."

" Child, you are right," said his father, after listening a moment; " the demons of the wilderness are gathered against the village, for human enemies make no such stir as this. We will ascend the great tree at once."

Thereupon he drew his wife out.

Kibatti wriggled himself through the burrow under the milk-weed hedge into the banana-grove, and having gained its deep shadows, raced for the great tree, closely followed by his parents. A large vine hung pendent, and up this vine Kibatti climbed, his mother after him, the old man last. Not a moment too soon, for just then the trumpet-note of the King Elephant was heard, and afterwards such a concert of noises that neither Kibatti nor his aged father had ever heard the like before. In the starlight they saw the huge forms of all kinds of furious animals pass and repass below them; but clinging closely to the shelter of the giant limbs of the tree, they, from their safe perch, witnessed the dreadful ending of their friends and relatives.

When he fully realized the catastrophe and its

completeness, Kibatti suggested to his parents that they should ascend to the very highest fork, lest they should be observed in the morning, and on climbing up they found a snug hiding-place far above, hidden all round by the thick, fleshy leaves of the tree. There they remained quiet until morning, when the boy's restless curiosity became so strong that he resolved to gratify it. Grasping close a great limb of the tree, he descended as far as the lower fork and looked down. He saw all the huts smashed, and the bones of his tribe white and gleaming, scattered about. The fences were all levelled, but the elephants, under their leader, were re-setting the poles round about. The lions were pacing watchfully around, the rhinoceroses and buffaloes were herded separately, gazing upon the elephants, the leopards were lying down under the trees in scattered groups, the hyenas were crunching bones, for these last never know when they have eaten enough.

Kibatti kept his post all day. By night the poles fenced the village round about as before, and in the dusk he saw the gathering together of all the creatures in a circle round the King Elephant, to hear his rumbling voice delivering an harangue to the motley allies. When it was ended the lions roared, the rhinoceroses snorted, the buffaloes bellowed, the hyenas laughed, and the shrill trumpetings of the elephants announced that the meeting was over. What occurred after, Kibatti did not stay to learn, but climbed aloft to give the news to his anxious parents.

Said he, "It appears to me, father, that they are going to build the village up again, for they have already fenced it around even better, as I think, than it was before. Those animals have clever leaders, that is certain, but I am not a man-son if Kibatti does not get the better of some of them."

"Oh, you are clever, my child, that is true," said the old man. "Whatever you undertake to do, done it is. I have found out that long ago. If wit will get us out of this place of danger, I have a conviction it will be by yours, and not by mine, or by my old woman's."

"I do not purpose to leave the tree just yet, father," replied Kibatti. "If we keep quiet, we could not find a safer place than here. The tree is so tall that they cannot hear us talk unless they set their ears to listen at the foot of it, and against all that may happen we must provide ourselves."

"Give your confidence to me, boy, and let me judge of your plan," said the father.

"Well, my idea is this. To-night they will all

start off, some to catch the lesser prey, others to
graze and feed. The leaders, of course, will
remain behind. I propose, after getting three or
four winks of sleep, to go down to the gate and
discover how things are. If possible, I will try
and get my net-ropes. They will be useful for
my purpose. We may trap some game, you
know."

" I see, I see, my boy. That is a good idea.
Shall I help you ? "

" Not to-night, father, except you keep watch
until yonder bright star stands overhead."

The old man agreed to keep watch until the
star approached the zenith. About midnight
Kibatti was waked, and having given his father
injunctions to go to sleep, he descended. He
proceeded straight to his house, and among the
wreckage he found his strong nets and their ropes,
and his sharp hunting-knife, besides his father's
five spears and his own quiver. These weapons he
conveyed directly to the tree, and bore them up to
the lower fork. This done, he re-descended the
tree and crawled away to a bit of marsh-land not
far off, where there was a crane's nest which contained some eggs. He took these in his hand, and
went around through the bushes to the Unyoro
Road. All this had been done very quickly,

because, being a hunter, he knew the neighbourhood well, and while watching the animals in the
village, his mind had been busy forming his plans.
Now when he came to the Unyoro Road, he stood
straight up and strode rapidly in the direction of
the village which had been that of his tribe's.
Arriving near it he crawled up to the gate and
looked in, then traced the fence all around until he
came back to the same gate.

Kibatti now stood up and hailed the animals,
crying loud,

"Hullo, hullo there! Are you all asleep?
Will ye not let a poor benighted stranger in?
The night is cold, and I am hungry."

King Buffalo, who was on guard, trotted up to
the gate, and looking out saw a small boy who was
naked, except for a scant robe which depended
from his shoulders.

"Who art thou?" demanded the buffalo in his
gruffest voice.

Kibatti answered in the thin voice of a fatherless
and starving orphan.

"It is I, Kibatti the Little, from Unyoro."

"What dost thou want?"

"Only a little fire to roast my eggs, and a place
to sleep. I am a forest-boy, and live alone in
Unyoro. My parents are both dead, and I have

no home.   If you will give me work I will stay
with you ; for then I shall have plenty to eat.   If

"IT IS I, KIBATTI THE LITTLE, FROM UNYORO."

not, let me sleep here to-night, and in the morning
I will go."

   "What work canst thou do ? "

   "Not much, but I can fetch water and fuel."

" Wait a minute ; I will see if our people will let thee in."

The buffalo moved away and woke up the rhinoceros, the elephant, the lion, the leopard, and hyena, and told them that there was a little forest-boy seeking a night's lodging. At first the general belief was, that he belonged to the tribe which had owned the village, but the buffalo denied that this boy could have known of the country, as he had come boldly up to the gate from the Unyoro road ; besides, was it likely that a small boy, knowing what had happened, would ever have come back when those who had destroyed the village were in possession of it. This last remark settled the matter. King Elephant said,

" As thou wilt, Buffalo. Even if the matter were otherwise, a small boy can do no harm. Let him in. We will give him plenty of work."

King Buffalo opened the gate and allowed Kibatti to enter, and introduced him to his friends, King Elephant and the rest, all of whom smiled as they saw his slender and small form, the only human amongst them. Buffalo took very kindly to his protégé, and showed him around, while Kibatti amused him with his innocent unsophisti-cated prattle, which convinced the kingly bovine that little Kibatti was indeed a wild-wood waif.

"And where do you all sleep?" asked Kibatti of Buffalo.

"I sleep here, near the gate, King Elephant rests near that big tree. King Lion prefers lying near that great log there, Brother Rhinoceros throws himself down on the edge of the banana grove, Leopard curls himself near the fence, and Hyena snores stupidly near his pile of bones."

After a little while Buffalo lay down near the gate for a little rest. Kibatti stretched himself near him, but not to sleep. His eyes were quite open, and he soon saw Buffalo's nose rest upon the ground and his head sway from side to side. Kibatti then untied a cord, and steathily passing it round the four legs of the buffalo, drew the other end round the neck in a slip noose without waking him. He then crawled off towards the elephant, and tied his four legs together, gently tightening the slip noose, and fastening the rope three or four times running round, and brought them all together. To the rhinoceros he did the same. He then went out of the gate and brought his bundle of nets. He took one up, fastened one end to the fence, and drawing it lightly like a curtain over the form of the sleeping lion, just hung it on splinters and projections of the fence. In like manner he secured a net over the leopard, and another over the hyena. All this did clever little Kibatti without waking any of them. He then stole out of the gate a second time, and made his way to the tree where his parents were sleeping.

" Come, father," he said, " the kings of the herds are trapped and netted. Bring down mother to the lower fork, and come, do you hasten with me with a bundle of spears, two bows, and quivers full of arrows, for we must finish the game before morning."

Completely armed with spears and arrows, Kibatti led his father to the gate, and stealthily entered the fenced enclosure, and they stood over the still-sleeping buffalo. Kibatti gave his father a sharp-pointed spear, and gently laying his finger on the vital spot, between neck and head, showed him where to strike. The father lifted his right arm high up, and with one stroke severed the spinal cord. A shiver passed through King Buffalo's body, and he rolled over stone dead.

Then Kibatti and his father approached King Lion, who lay lengthways near the log by the fence, with his side exposed. Kibatti pointed to his own left side behind the shoulder-blade, and father and son drew their bows and drove two arrows into Lion's heart, who sprang up and threw himself like a ball into the net, which closed round him taut, and he presently lay still and lifeless. In the same manner father and son despatched Leopard and Hyena. There then only remained Rhinoceros and Elephant.

They chose to attack the first-named beast, who was still lying down on his side, unconscious of the tragic fate of his confederates.

KILLING KING RHINOCEROS.

Kibatti pointed to the enemy's fore-shoulder and touched his father with his finger two inches below the shoulder-blade. His father understood, and launched his spear straight into the body with such force that the blade was buried. King Rhinoceros, feeling the iron in his vitals, snorted and struggled to stand, but in doing so tightened the cords, and fell back rolling half over. Kibatti drew his bow and buried an arrow close to his father's buried spear. Meantime, King Elephant had taken the alarm, and, struggling with his bonds, had capsized himself on the ground.

Kibatti gave vent to a war whoop and cried :

"Never mind, father, let the rhinoceros die. Let us away to the elephant while he is helpless."

They sprang to the prostrate beast, and they shot their arrows first to every vital point exposed, and then launched their spears with such good effect that before long the last of the kings of the beasts had ended his life.

Kibatti and his father then flew to where the old woman crouched in the fork of the tree, and taking her with them, they left the ruined village, and sought a home in another district, where, because of the terrible revenge they had taken on the forest lords, they were held by their fellow-creatures all their lives in great esteem.

THE PARTNERSHIP OF RABBIT AND ELEPHANT, AND WHAT CAME OF IT.

WHILE going to the Albert Edward Nyanza in 1876, Sabadu and Bujomba and others of our Waganda escort would join us at our evening fire, and when they found what entertainment was to be had, they readily yielded to the invitation to contribute their share to it. Besides, Sabadu was unequalled in the art of storytelling: he was fluent and humorous, while his mimicry of the characters he described kept everybody's interest on the alert. To the Rabbit of course he gave a wee thin voice, to the Elephant he gave a deep bass, to the Buffalo a hollow mooing. When he attempted the Lion, the veins of his temple and neck were dreadfully distended as he made the effort ; but when he mimicked the dog, one almost expected a little terrier-like dog to trot up to the fire, so perfect was his yaup-yaup.

Every one agreed as Sabadu began his story that his manner, even his style of sitting and smoothing his face, the pose of his head, betrayed the man of practice. The following is his story :—

In Willimesi, Uganda, a Rabbit and an Elephant, coming from different directions, met on a road one day, and being old friends, stopped to greet one another, and chat about the weather and the crops, and to exchange opinions on the state of trade. Finally the Rabbit proposed that the Elephant should join him in a partnership to make a little trading expedition to the Watusi shepherds, " because," said he, " I hear there are some good chances to make profit among them. Cloth, I am told, is very scarce there, and I think we might find a good bargain awaiting us." The Elephant was nothing loth, and closed with the offer of his little friend, and a couple of bales of assorted goods were prepared for the journey.

They set out on particularly good terms with each other, and Rabbit, who had a good store of experiences, amused the Elephant greatly. By-and-by the pair of friends arrived at a river, and the Elephant, to whom the water was agreeable, stepped in to cross it, but halted on hearing Rabbit exclaim :

" Why, Elephant, you surely are not going to cross without me ?   Are we not partners ? "

" Of course we are partners, but I did not agree to carry you or your pack.   Why don't you step right in ?   The water is not deep, it scarcely covers my feet."

" But, you stupid fellow, can you not see that what will scarcely cover your feet is more than enough to drown me, and I can't swim a bit ; and, besides, if I get my fur wet I shall catch the ague, and how ever am I to carry my pack across ? "

" Well, I cannot help that.   It was you who proposed to take the journey, and I thought a wise fellow like you would have known that there were rivers running across the road, and that you knew what to do.   If you cannot travel, then good-bye. I cannot stop here all day," and the Elephant walked on across to the other side.

" Surly rascal," muttered Rabbit.   " All right, my big friend, I will pay you for it some time."

Not far off, however, Rabbit found a log, and after placing his pack on it, he paddled himself over, and reached the other bank safely ; but to his grief he discovered that his bale had been wetted and damaged.

Rabbit wiped the water up as much as possible, and resumed the journey with the Elephant, who had looked carelessly on the efforts of his friend to cross the river.

Fortunately for Rabbit, the latter part of the journey did not present such difficulties, and they arrived in due time among the Watusi shepherds.

Now at a trade Elephant was not to be compared with Rabbit, for he could not talk so pleasantly as Rabbit, and he was not at all sociable. Rabbit went among the women, and laughed and joked with them, and said so many funny things, that they were delighted with him, and when at last the trade question was cautiously touched upon, a chief's wife was so kind to him, that she gave a mighty fine cow in exchange for his little bale of cloth. Elephant, on the other hand, went among the men, and simply told them that he had come to buy cattle with cloth. The Watusi shepherds, not liking his appearance or his manner, said they had no cattle to sell, but if he cared to have it, they would give a year-old heifer for his bale. Though Elephant's bale was a most weighty one, and many times more valuable than Rabbit's, yet as he was so gruff and ugly, he was at last obliged to be satisfied with the little heifer.

Just as they had left the Watusi to begin their return journey, Elephant said to Rabbit, " Now mind, should we meet anyone on the road, and we are asked whose cattle these are, I wish you to oblige me by saying that they are mine, because I should not like people to believe that I am not as good a trader as yourself. They will also be afraid to touch them if they know they belong to me ; whereas, if they hear that they belong to you, every fellow will think he has as good a right to them as yourself, and you dare not defend your property."

" Very well," replied Rabbit, " I quite understand."

In a little while, as Rabbit and Elephant drove their cattle along, they met many people coming from market who stopped and admired them, and said, " Ah, what a fine cow is that ! to whom does it belong ? "

" It belongs to me," answered the thin voice of Rabbit. " The little one belongs to Elephant."

" Very fine indeed. A good cow that," replied the people, and passed on.

Vexed and annoyed, Elephant cried angrily to Rabbit, " Why did you not answer as I told you ? Now mind, do as I tell you at the next meeting with strangers."

" Very well," answered Rabbit, " I will try and remember."

By-and-by they met another party going home with fowls and palm wine, who, when they came up, said, " Ah that is a fine beast, and in prime order.   Whose is it ? "

" It is mine," quickly replied Rabbit, " and the little scabby heifer belongs to Elephant."

This answer enraged Elephant, who said, " What an obstinate little fool you are.   Did you not hear me ask you to say it was mine ?   Now, remember, you are to say so next time, or I leave you to find your own way home, because I know you are a horrible little coward."

" Very well, I'll do it next time," replied Rabbit in a meek voice.

In a short time they met another crowd, which stopped when opposite to them, and the people said, " Really, that is an exceedingly fine cow.   To which of you does it belong ? "

" It is mine.   I bought it from the Watusi," replied Rabbit.

The Elephant was so angry this time, that he broke away from Rabbit, and drove his little heifer by another road, and to Lion, and Hyena, and Buffalo, and Leopard, whom he met, he said what a fine fat cow was being driven by cowardly little

Rabbit along the other road. He did this out of mere spite, hoping that some one of them would be tempted to take it by force from Rabbit.

But Rabbit was wise, and had seen the spite in Elephant's face as he went off, and was sure that he would play him some unkind trick ; and, as night was falling and his home was far, and he knew that there were many vagabonds lying in wait to rob poor travellers, he reflected that if his wit failed to save him he would be in great danger.

True enough, it was not long before a big blustering lion rose from the side of the road, and cried out, "Hello, you there. Where are you going with that cow? Come, speak out."

"Ah, is that you, Lion? I am taking it to Mugassa (the deity), who is about to give a feast to all his friends, and he told me particularly to invite you to share it, if I should meet you."

"Eh? What? To Mugassa? Oh, well, I am proud to have met you, Rabbit. As I am not otherwise engaged I will accompany you, because everyone considers it an honour to wait upon Mugassa."

They proceeded a little further, and a bouncing buffalo came up and bellowed fiercely. "You, Rabbit, stop," said he. "Where are you taking that cow to?"

" I am taking it to Mugassa, don't you know. How would a little fellow like me have the courage to go so far from home if it were not that I am on

"I AM PROUD TO HAVE MET YOU, RABBIT."

service for Mugassa. I am charged also to tell you, Buffalo, that if you like to join in the feast Mugassa is about to give, that he will be glad to have you as a guest."

" Oh, well, that is good news indeed. I will come along now, Rabbit, and am very glad to have met you. How do you do, Lion ? "

A short distance off the party met a huge rogue elephant, who stood in the middle of the road, and demanded to know where the cow was being taken in a tone which required a quick answer.

" Now, Elephant, get out of the way. This cow is being taken to Mugassa, who will be angry with you if I am delayed. Have you not heard of the feast he is about to give ? By the bye, as you are one of the guests, you might as well help me to drive this cow, and let me get on your back, for I am dreadfully tired."

" Why, that's grand," said the Elephant. " I shall be delighted to feast with Mugassa, and—come get on my back. I will carry you with pleasure. And, Rabbit," whispered Elephant, as he lifted him by his trunk, " don't forget to speak a good word for me to Mugassa."

Soon a leopard and then a hyena were met, but seeing such a powerful crowd behind the cow, they affected great civility, and were invited to accompany Rabbit's party to Mugassa's feast.

It was quite dark by the time they arrived at Rabbit's village. At the gate stood two dogs, who were Rabbit's chums, and they barked furiously ;

but hearing their friend's voice, they came up and welcomed Rabbit.

The party halted, and Rabbit, after reaching the ground, whispered to Dogs how affairs stood, and Dogs wagged their tails approvingly, and yauped with fun as they heard of Rabbit's wit. It did not

" A POWERFUL CROWD BEHIND THE COW."

take long for Dogs to understand what was required of them, and one of them bounded off to the village, and after a short time returned with a pretended message from the great Mugassa.

" Well, my friends, do you hear what Mugassa says ? " cried Rabbit, with a voice of importance.

" Dogs are to lay mats inside the village by the

gate, and the cow is to be killed, and the meat prepared nicely and laid on the mats. And when that is
done, Mugassa himself will come and give each his
portion. He says that you are all very welcome."

" Now listen to me before I go in to Mugassa, and
I will show you how you can all help to hurry the
feast, for I am sure you are all anxious to begin."

" You, Hyena, you must kill the cow, and dress
the meat, and Dogs will carry it in and lay it on
the mats ; but remember, if a bit is touched before
Mugassa commands, we are all ruined."

" You, Elephant, you take this brass hatchet of
Mugassa's, and split wood nicely for the hearth."

" Buffalo, you go and find a wood with a smooth
bark and which burns well, and bring it to
Elephant."

" Leopard, you go to the banana plantations, and
watch for a falling leaf and catch it with your eye-
lids in order that we may have a proper plate for
Mugassa.

" Lion, my friend, do you go and fill this pot from
the spring, and bring water that Mugassa may
wash his hands."

Having issued his instructions, Rabbit went
strutting into the village ; but after he had gone a
little way he darted aside, and passing through a
side door, went out and came creeping up towards

an ant-hill. On the top was a tuft of grass, and from his hiding-place he commanded a view of the gate, and of all who might come near it.

Now Buffalo could only find one log with smooth bark, and Dogs shouted out to Buffalo that one log was not enough to roast or to boil the meat, and he returned to hunt up some more.

Elephant struck the log with his brass hatchet, which was broken at the first blow, and there was nothing else with which to cut the wood.

Leopard watched and watched for falling leaves, but failed to see any.

Lion's pot had a hole in the bottom, and he could never keep it full, though he tried ever so many times.

Meanwhile Hyena having killed the cow and dressed the meat beautifully, said to Dogs, " Now my friends, the meat is ready. What shall I do."

" You can help us carry the meat in, and lay it on the mats, if you like, for Mugassa must see it before anybody can touch it."

" Ah, but I feel extremely hungry, and my mouth waters so that I am sick with longing. May we not go shares and eat a little bit ? It looks very nice and fat," whined the Hyena.

" Ah, no, we should not dare do such a thing. We have long ago left the woods, and its habits, and are unfit for anything but human society ; but if you were allowed to eat any, you could fly into the woods, and we should have all the blame. No, no, come, help us carry it inside. You will not have to wait long."

The Hyena was obliged to obey, but contrived to hide in the grass some of the tripe. Rabbit, from behind his tuft of grass, saw it all, and winked in the dark.

When the meat was in, Dogs said, "It is all right now. Just stay outside until the other fellows arrive."

Hyena retired, and when he was outside of the gate searched for his tripe, and lay down quietly to enjoy it, but as he was about to bite it, Rabbit screamed, "Ah, you thief, Hyena. You thief, I see you. Stop thief, Mugassa is coming."

These cries so alarmed Hyena that he dropped his tripe, and fled away as fast as his legs could carry him, and the others, Buffalo, Elephant, Lion, and Leopard, tired out with waiting, and hearing these alarming cries, also ran away, leaving Rabbit and his dog friends in quiet possession. They carried the tripe into the village, and closed the gate and barred it, after which they laughed loud and long, Rabbit rolling on the ground over and over with the fun of it all.

"FLED AWAY AS FAST AS THEIR LEGS COULD CARRY THEM."

My friends, Rabbit was the smallest of all, but by his wisdom he was more than a match for two Elephants, Buffalo, Leopard, Lion, Hyena, and all. And even his friends, the Dogs, had to confess that Rabbit's wit could not be matched. That is my tale.

THE ADVENTURES OF SARUTI.

" I HAVE a poor memory for legends," said Bujomba, one night, while we were in camp at Benga: " but I remember what a young Mtongolè (colonel) named Saruti related to Mtesa after his return from an expedition to the frontier of Unyoro. What a head that man had, and such eyes ! Mtesa was ever fond of a good story, and loved to question those whom he sent to distant countries, until you might say that there was nothing left in a man worth hearing after he had done with him. But Saruti did not need any questioning. He talked on and on without stopping, until Mtesa could not sit up longer for sheer weariness. These are among the things he said that he had witnessed

on his journey. You must not ask me if I believe
all that he said. All I can say is that they might
have happened, or been seen by many men, but I
never could quite understand how it was that
Saruti alone was so lucky as to see all the things
he talked about. Anyhow, he was very amusing,
and Mtesa laughed heartily many times as he
listened to him."

Kabaka, I think my charms which my father
suspended round my neck must be very powerful.
I am always in luck. I hear good stories on my
journey, I see strange things which no one else
seems to have come across. Now on this last
journey, by the time I reached Singo, I came to a
little village, and as I was drinking banana wine
with the chief, he told me that there were two
lions near his village who had a band of hyenas to
serve as soldiers under them. They used to send
them out in pairs, sometimes to one district, and
sometimes to another, to purvey food for them.
If the peasants showed fight, they went back and
reported to their masters, and the lions brought
all their soldiers with them, who bothered them so
that they were glad to leave a fat bullock tied to
a tree as tribute. Then the lions would take the
bullock and give orders that the peasant who paid
his tribute should be left in peace. The chief

declared this to be a fact, having had repeated proof of it.

At the next place, which is Mbagwè, the man Buvaiya, who is in charge, told me that when he went a short time before to pay his respects to the Muzimu (the oracle) of the district, he met about thirty *kokorwa* on the road, hunting close together for snakes, and that as soon as they saw him, they charged at him, and would have killed him had he not run up a tree. He tells me that though they are not much bigger than rabbits, they are very savage, and make travelling alone very dangerous. I think they must be some kind of small dogs. Perhaps the old men of the court may be better able to tell you what they are.

At the next village of Ngondo a smart boy called Rutuana was brought to me, who was said to have been lately playing with a young friend of the same age at long stick and little stick (tipcat ?). His friend hit the little stick, and sent it a great way, and Rutuana had to fetch it from the long grass. While searching for it, one of those big serpents which swallow goats and calves caught him, and coiled itself around him. Though he screamed out for help, Rutuana laid his stick across his chest, and clutching hold of each end with a hand, held fast to it until help came. His

friend ran up a tree, and only helped him by
screaming. As the serpent could not break the boy's
hold of the stick, he was unable to crush his ribs,

"RUTUANA LAID HIS STICK ACROSS HIS CHEST."

because his outstretched arms protected them; but
when he was nearly exhausted the villagers came out
with spears and shields. These fellows, however,
were so stupid that they did not know how to kill

the serpent until Rutuana shouted to them: "Quick! draw your bows and shoot him through the neck." A man stepped forward then, and when close to him pierced his throat with the arrow, and as the serpent uncoiled himself to attack the men, Rutuana fell down. The serpent was soon speared, and the boy was carried home. I think that boy will become a great warrior.

At the next village the peasants were much disturbed by a multitude of snakes which had collected there for some reason. They had seen several long black snakes which had taken lodging in the ant-hills. These had already killed five cows, and lately had taken to attacking the travellers along the road that leads by the ant-hills, when an Arab, named Massoudi, hearing of their trouble, undertook to kill them. He had some slaves with him, and he clothed their legs with buffalo hide, and placed cooking-pots on their heads, and told them to go among the ant-hills. When the snakes came out of their holes he shot them one by one. Among the reptiles he killed were three kinds of serpents which possessed horns. The peasants skinned them, and made bags of them to preserve their charms. One kind of horned snake, very thick and short, is said to lay eggs as large as those of fowls. The *mubarasassa*,

which is of a greyish colour, is also said to be able
to kill elephants.

I then went to Kyengi, beyond Singo, and the
peasants, on coming to gossip with me, rather
upset me with terrible stories of the mischief done
by a big black leopard. It seems that he had
first killed a woman, and had carried the body into
the bush ; and another time had killed two men
while they were setting their nets for some small
ground game. Then a native hunter, under
promise of reward from the chief, set out with
two spears to kill him. He did not succeed, but
he said that he saw a strange sight. As he was
following the track of the leopard, he suddenly
came to a little jungle, with an open space in the
middle. A large wild sow, followed by her litter
of little pigs, was rooting about, and grunting as
pigs do, when he saw the monstrous black leopard
crawl towards one of the pigs. Then there was a
shrill squeal from a piggie, and the mother, looking
up, discovered its danger, at which it furiously
charged the leopard, clashing her tusks and
foaming at the mouth. The leopard turned sharp
round, and sprang up a tree. The sow tried to
jump up after it, but being unable to reach her
enemy in that way, she set about working hard at
the roots. While she was busy about it the

peasant ran back to obtain a net and assistants, and to get his hunting-dog. When he returned, the sow was still digging away at the bottom of the tree, and had made a great hole all round it. The pigs, frightened at seeing so many men, trotted away into the bush, and the hunter and his friends prepared to catch the leopard. They pegged the net all about the tree, then let loose the dog, and urged him towards the net. As he touched the net, the hunters made a great noise, and shouted, at which the leopard bounded from the tree, and with one scratch of his paw ripped the dog open, sprang over the net, tapped one of the men on the shoulder, and was running away, when he received a wound in the shoulder, and stopped to bite the spear. The hunters continued to worry him, until at last, covered with blood, he lay down and died.

One day's journey beyond Kyengi, I came to the thorn-fenced village of some Watusi shepherds, who, it seems, had suffered much from a pair of lion cubs, which were very fierce. The headman's little boy was looking after some calves when the cubs came and quietly stalked him through the grass, and caught him. The headman took it so much to heart, that as soon as he heard the news he went straight back to his village and hanged

"TRIED TO JUMP UP AFTER THE LEOPARD."

himself to a rafter. The Watusi love their families
very much, but it seems to be a custom with these
herdsmen that if a man takes his own life, the
body cannot be buried, and though he was a
headman, they carried it to the jungle, and after
leaving it for the vultures, they returned and set
fire to his hut, and burnt it to the ground. When
they had done that, the Watusi collected together
and had a long hunt after the young lions, but as
yet they have not been able to find them.

When the sun was half way up the sky, I came
from Kyengi to some peasants, who lived near a
forest which is affected by the man-monkeys
called nziké (gorilla ?). I was told by them that
the nziké know how to smoke and make fire just
as we do. It is a custom among the natives, when
they see smoke issuing through the trees, for them
to say, " Behold, the nziké is cooking his food."
I asked them if it were true that the nziké carried
off women to live with them, but they all told
me that it was untrue, though the old men sometimes tell such stories to frighten the women, and
keep them at home out of danger. Knowing that
I was on the king's business, they did not dare tell
me their fables.

By asking them all sorts of questions, I was
shown to a very old man with a white beard, with

whom I obtained much amusement. It appears he is a great man at riddles, and he asked me a great many.

One was, " What is it that always goes straight ahead, and never looks back ? "

I tried hard to answer him, but when finally he announced that it was a river, I felt very foolish.

He then asked me, " What is it that is bone outside and meat within ? "

The people laughed, and mocked me. Then he said that it was an egg, which was very true.

Another question he gave me was, " What is it that looks both ways when you pass it ? "

Some said one thing, and some said another, and at last he answered that it was grass.

Then he asked me, " What good thing was it which a man eats, and which he constantly fastens his eyes upon while he eats, and after eating, throws a half away ? " I thought and considered, but I never knew what it was until he told me that it was a roasted ear of Indian corn.

That old man was a very wise one, and among some of his sayings was that " When people dream much, the old moon must be dying."

He also said that " When the old moon is dying, the hunter need never leave home to seek game,

because it is well known that he would meet
nothing."

And he further added, that at that time the
potter need not try to bake any pots, because the
clay would be sure to be rotten.

Some other things which he said made me think
a little of their meaning.

He said, " When people have provisions in their
huts, they do not say, Let us go into another man's
house and rob him."

He also said, " When you see a crookback, you
do not ask him to stand straight, nor an old man to
join the dance, nor the man who is in pain, to
laugh."

And what he said about the traveller is very true.
" The man who clings to his own hearth does not
tickle our ears, like him who sees many lands, and
hears new stories."

The next day I stopped at a village near the
little lake of Kitesa's called Mtukura. The chief
in charge loved talking so much, that he soon made
me as well acquainted with the affairs of his family
as though he courted my sister. His people are
accustomed to eat frogs and rats, and from the noise
in the reeds, and the rustling and squealings in
the roof of the hut I slept in, I think there is
little fear of famine in that village. Nor are they

averse, they tell me, to iguanas and those vile feeders, the hyenas.

It is a common belief in the country that it was Naraki, a wife of Uni, a sultan of Unyoro, who made that lake. While passing through, she was very thirsty, and cried out to her Muzimu (spirit ?), the Muzimu which attends the kings of Unyoro, and which are most potent. And all at once there was a hissing flight of firestones (meteorites ?) in the air, and immediately after, there was a fall of a monstrously large one, which struck the ground close to her, and made a great hole, out of which the water spurted and continued leaping up until a lake was formed, and buried the fountain out of sight, and the rising waters formed a river, which has run north from the lake ever since into the Kafu.

Close by this lake is a dark grove, sacred to Muzingeh, the king of the birds. It is said that he has only one eye, but once a year he visits the grove, and after building his house, he commands all the birds from the Nyanzas and the groves, to come and see him and pay their homage. For half a moon the birds, great and small, may be seen following him about along the shores of the lake, like so many guards around a king ; and before night they are seen returning in

the same manner to the grove. The parrots' cries
tell the natives when they come, and no one would
care to miss the sight, and the glad excitement
among the feathered tribe. But there is one bird,
called the Kirurumu, that refuses to acknowledge the
sovereignty of the Muzingeh. The other birds have
tried often to induce him to associate with the
Muzingeh ; but Kirurumu always answers that a
beautiful creature like himself, with gold and blue
feathers, and such a pretty crest, was never meant
to be seen in the company of an ugly bird that
possesses only one eye.

On the other side of Lake Mtukura is a forest
where Dungu, the king of the animals, lives. It is
to Dungu that all the hunters pray when they set
out to seek for game. He builds first a small hut,
and after propitiating him with a small piece of
flesh, he asks Dungu, that he may be successful.
Then Dungu enters into the hunter's head, if he is
pleased with the offering, and the cunning of the
man becomes great ; his nerves stiffen, and his
bowels are strengthened, and the game is secured.
When Dungu wishes a man to succeed in the hunt,
it is useless for the buffalo to spurn the earth and
moo, or for the leopard to cover himself with sand
in his rage—the spear of the hunter drinks his
blood. But the hunter must not forget to pay the

tribute to the deity, lest he be killed on the way home.

The friendly chief insisted that I should become his blood-fellow, and stay with him a couple of days. The witch-doctor, a man of great influence in the country, was asked to unite us. He took a sharp little knife, and made a gash in the skin of my right leg, just above the knee, and did the same to the chief, and then rubbed his blood over my wound, and my blood over his, and we became brothers. Among his gifts was this beautiful shield, which I beg Mtesa, my Kabaka, to accept, because I have seen none so beautiful, and it is too good for a colonel whose only hope and wish is to serve his king.

I am glad that I rested there, because I saw a most wonderful sight towards evening. As we were seated under the bananas, we heard a big he-goat's bleat, and by the sound of it we knew that it was neither for fun nor for love. It was a tone of anger and fear. Almost at the same time, one of the boys rushed up to us, and his face had really turned grey from fear, and he cried, " There is a lion in the goat-pen, and the big he-goat is fighting with him." They had forgotten to tell me about this famous goat, which was called Kasuju, after some great man who had been renowned in war, and he certainly was worth speaking about, and

Kasuju was well known round about for his wonderful strength and fighting qualities. When we got near the pen with our spears and shields, the he-goat was butting the lion—who was young, for he had no mane—as he might have butted a pert young nanny-goat, and baaing with as full a note as that of a buffalo calf. It appears that Kasuju saw the destroyer creeping towards one of his wives, and dashing at his flank knocked him down. As we looked on from the outside, we saw that Kasuju was holding his own very well, and we thought that we would not check the fight, but prepare ourselves to have a good cast at the lion as he attempted to leave. The lion was getting roused up, and we saw the spring he made : but Kasuju nimbly stept aside and gave him such a stroke that it sounded like a drum. Then Kasuju trotted away in front of his trembling wives, and as the lion came up, we watched him draw his ears back as he raised himself on his hind feet like a warrior. The lion advanced to him, and he likewise rose as though he would wrestle with him, when Kasuju shot into his throat with so true and fair a stroke, that drove one of his horns deep into the throat. It was then the lion's claws began to work, and with every scratch poor Kasuju's hide was torn dreadfully, but he kept his horn in the wound, and pushed home, and made the wound large. Then the lion sprang free, and the blood spurted all over Kasuju. Blinded with his torn and hanging scalp, and weakened with his wounds, he staggered about, pounding blindly at its enemy, until the lion gave him one mighty stroke with its paw, and sent him headlong, and then seized him by the neck and shook him, and we heard the cruel crunch as the fangs met. But it was the last effort of the lion, for just as Kasuju was lifeless, the lion rolled over him dead also. Had my friend told me this story, I should not have believed him, but as I saw it with my own eyes, I am bound to believe it. We buried Kasuju honourably in a grave, as we would bury a brave man ; but the lion we skinned, and I have got his fur with the ragged hole in the throat.

The singular fight we had witnessed, furnished us all with much matter for talk about lions, and it brought into the mind of one of them a story of a crocodile and lion fight which had happened some time before in the night. Lake Mtukura swarms with crocodiles, and situated as it is in a region of game they must be fat with prey. One night a full-grown lion with a fine mane came to cool his dry throat in the lake, and was quaffing water, when he felt his nose seized by something that rose up from below.

From the traces of the struggle by the water's edge, it must have been a terrible one. The crocodile's long claws had left deep marks, showing how he must have been lifted out of the water, and flung forcibly down ; but in the morning both lion and crocodile were found dead, the crocodile's throat

" FELT HIS NOSE SEIZED."

wide open with a broad gash, but his teeth still fastened in the lion's nose.

Saruti had not half finished his stories when he felt, by seeing Mtesa yawn, that though his adventures were very interesting, and he was quite ready to continue, yet it would be to his advantage to dock his tongue for the time being. So he said, "Kabaka, the wise old man whom I met, told me one thing I had nearly forgotten to say. He said, " I know you are a servant of the king, and if ever you want the king's face to soften to you and his hand to open with gifts, compare yourself to the lid of a cooking-pot, which, though the pot may be full of fragrant stew, receives naught but the vapour, and the king who is wise will understand and will be pleased with his servant."

" Very well said indeed, Saruti," cried Mtesa, laughing. " I understand. The lid must share with the pot this time. Steward," he said, turning to Kauta, " see that six head of cattle be driven to Saruti's cattle-pen ; " and Saruti twiyanzied (thanked with prostrations) so often that his head swam.

THE BOY KINNENEH AND THE GORILLA.

IT is in such stories as the Fable of the Rabbit, the Leopard and the Goat, the Dog and the little Chicken, the Leopard, the Sheep and the Dove, the Crane, the Leopard and the Sheep, the Rabbit and the Lion, the Cow and the Lion, the Lion and his mane, the Rabbit and the Leopard, and the boy Kinneneh and the Gorilla, that Kadu, our accomplished relator of legends, shone. It is not with a wish to be unkind to Kadu that I say he showed only too well that according to him cunning was to be preferred to strength. Perhaps he was right, though cunning is a word in much discredit with us nowadays, because we are accustomed to ally

it with deception and fraud, but we will put
the best possible construction on it out of admiration for and gratitude to Kadu, and claim that
his cunning, which was the moral of most of his
stories, was a kind of illegitimate wisdom, or a
permissible artfulness. None of us, at least, but
sympathised with Kadu's dumb heroes when by a
little pleasant cheat or sly stratagem, the bullying
buffalo got the worst of an encounter with the sharp-
witted rabbit, or when the dog got the better
of his sour mistress the leopardess, or when rabbit
put to shame the surly elephant, or when Kibatti
conquered the kings of the animal tribes. The
legend of Kinneneh and the Gorilla was another
story which evidently was meant by Kadu and the
unknown ancient of Uganda who invented it to
illustrate that cunning is mightier than strength.
He told it in this wise :

In the early days of Uganda, there was a small
village situate on the other side of the Katonga, in
Buddu, and its people had planted bananas and
plantains which in time grew to be quite a large
grove, and produced abundant and very fine fruit.
From a grove of bananas when its fruit is ripe
there comes a very pleasant odour, and when a
puff of wind blows over it, and bears the fragrance
towards you, I know of nothing so well calculated

to excite the appetite, unless it be the smell of roasted meat. Anyhow, such must have been the feeling of a mighty big gorilla, who one day, while roaming about alone in the woods searching for nuts to eat, suddenly stopped and stood up and sniffed for some time, with his nose well out in the direction of the village. But shaking his head he fell on all fours again to resume his search for food. Again there came with a whiff of wind a strong smell of ripe bananas, and he stood on his feet once more, and with his nose shot out thus he drew in a greedy breath and then struck himself over the stomach, and said :

" I thought it was so. There are bananas that way, and I must get some."

Down he fell on all fours, and put out his arms with long stretches, just as a fisherman draws in a heavy net, and is eager to prevent the escape of the fish.

In a little while he came to the edge of the grove, and stood and looked gloatingly on the beautiful fruit hanging in great bunches. Presently he saw something move. It was a woman bent double over a basket, and packing the fruit neatly in it, so that she could carry a large quantity at one journey.

The gorilla did not stay long thinking, but

crawled up secretly to her; and then with open
arms rushed forward and seized her. Before the
woman could utter her alarm he had lifted her and
her basket and trotted away with them into the
deepest bush. On reaching his den he flung the
woman on the ground, as you would fling dead
meat, and bringing the banana basket close to him,
his two legs hugging it close to his round paunch,
he began to gorge himself, muttering while he
peeled the fruit strange sounds. By-and-by the
woman came to her senses, but instead of keeping
quiet, she screamed and tried to run away. If it
were not for that movement and noise, she perhaps
might have been able to creep away unseen, but
animals of all kinds never like to be disturbed
while eating, so Gorilla gave one roar of rage, and
gave her such a squeeze that the breath was clean
driven out of her. When she was still he fell to
again, and tore the peeling off the bananas, and
tossed one after another down his wide throat,
until there was not one of the fruit left in the
basket, and the big paunch was swollen to twice
its first size. Then, after laying his paw on the
body to see if there was any life left in it, he
climbed up to his nest above, and curled himself
into a ball for a sleep.

When he woke he shook himself and yawned,

HE LIFTED THE WOMAN AND HER BASKET AND TROTTED
AWAY.

and looking below he saw the body of the woman, and her empty basket, and he remembered what had happened. He descended the tree, lifted the body and let it fall, then took up the basket, looked inside and outside of it, raked over the peelings of the bananas, but could not find anything left to eat.

He began to think, scratching the fur on his head, on his sides, and his paunch, picking up one thing and then another in an absent-minded way. And then he appeared to have made up a plan.

Whatever it was, this is what he did. It was still early morning, and as there was no sign of a sun, it was cold, and human beings must have been finishing their last sleep. He got up and went straight for the plantation. On the edge of the banana grove he heard a cock crow; he stopped and listened to it; he became angry.

" Some one," he said to himself, " is stealing my bananas," and with that he marched in the direction where the cock was crowing.

He came to the open place in front of the village, and saw several tall houses much larger than his own nest; and while he was looking at them, the door of one of them was opened, and a man came out. He crept towards him, and before he could

cry out the gorilla had squeezed him until his ribs
had cracked, and he was dead ; he flung him down,
and entered into the hut. He there saw a woman,
who was blowing a fire on the hearth, and he took
hold of her and squeezed her until there was no
life left in her body. There were three children
inside, and a bed on the floor. He treated them also
in the same way, and they were all dead. Then
he went into another house, and slew all the people
in it, one with a squeeze, another with a squeeze
and a bite with his great teeth, and there was not
one left alive. In this way he entered into five
houses and killed all the people in them, but in the
sixth house lived the boy Kinneneh and his old
mother.

Kinneneh had fancied that he heard an unusual
sound, and he had stood inside with his eyes close to
a chink in the reed door for some time when he saw
something that resembled what might be said to be
half animal and half man. He walked like a man,
but had the fur of a beast. His arms were long, and
his body was twice the breadth and thickness of a
full-grown man. He did not know what it was,
and when he saw it go into his neighbours' houses,
and heard those strange sounds, he grew afraid,
and turned and woke his mother, saying,

"Mother, wake up ! there is a strange big beast

in our village killing our people. So wake up quickly and follow me."

"But whither shall we fly, my son?" she whispered anxiously.

"Up to the loft, and lie low in the darkest place," replied Kinneneh, and he set her the example and assisted his mother.

Now those Uganda houses are not low-roofed like these of Congo-land, but are very high, as high as a tree, and they rise to a point, and near the top there is a loft where we stow our nets, and pots, and where our spear-shafts and bows are kept to season, and where our corn is kept to dry, and green bananas are stored to ripen. It was in this dark lofty place that Kinneneh hid himself and his mother, and waited in silence.

In a short time the gorilla put his head into their house and listened, and stepping inside he stood awhile, and looked searchingly around. He could see no one and heard nothing stir. He peered under the bed-grass, into the black pots and baskets, but there was no living being to be found.

"Ha, ha," he cried, thumping his chest like a man when he has got the big head. "I am the boss of this place now, and the tallest of these human nests shall be my own, and I shall feast

every day on ripe bananas and plantains, and
there is no one who can molest me—ha, ha!"

" Ha, ha!" echoed a shrill, piping voice after his
great bass.

The gorilla looked around once more, among the
pots, and the baskets, but finding nothing walked
out. Kinneneh, after awhile skipped down the
ladder and watched between the open cane-work of
the door, and saw him enter the banana-grove, and
waited there until he returned with a mighty load
of the fruit. He then saw him go out again into
the grove, and bidding his mother lie still and
patient, Kinneneh slipped out and ascended into
the loft of the house chosen by the gorilla for his
nest, where he hid himself and waited.

Presently the gorilla returned with another load
of the fruit, and, squatting on his haunches, commenced to peel the fruit, and fill his throat and
mouth with it, mumbling and chuckling, and
saying,

" Ha, ha! This is grand! Plenty of bananas
to eat, and all—all my own. None to say, 'Give
me some,' but all my very own. Ho, ho! I shall
feast every day. Ha, ha!"

" Ha, ha," echoed the piping voice again.

The gorilla stopped eating and made an ugly
frown as he listened. Then he said :

" That is the second time I have heard a thin voice saying, ' Ha, ha!' If I only knew who he was that cried ' Ha, ha!' I would squeeze him, and squeeze him until he cried, ' Ugh, ugh!' "

" Ugh, ugh!" echoed the little voice again.

The gorilla leaped to his feet and rummaged around the pots and the baskets, took hold of the bodies one after another and dashed them against the floor, then went to every house and searched, but could not discover who it was that mocked him.

In a short time he returned and ate a pile of bananas that would have satisfied twenty men, and afterwards he went out, saying to himself that it would be a good thing to fill the nest with food, as it was a bore to leave the warm nest each time he felt a desire to eat.

No sooner had he departed than Kinneneh slipped down, and carried every bunch that had been left away to his own house, where they were stowed in the loft for his mother, and after enjoining his mother to remain still, he waited, peering through the chinks of the door.

He soon saw gorilla bearing a pile of bunches that would have required ten men to carry, and, after flinging them into the chief's house, return to the plantation for another supply. While Gorilla was tearing down the plants and plucking at the bunches, Kinneneh was actively engaged in transferring what he brought into the loft by his mother's side. Gorilla made many trips in this manner, and brought in great heaps, but somehow his stock appeared to be very small. At last his strength was exhausted, and feeling that he could do no more that day, he commenced to feed on what he had last brought, promising to himself that he would do better in the morning.

At dawn the gorilla hastened out to obtain a supply of fruit for his breakfast, and Kinneneh took advantage of his absence to hide himself overhead.

He was not long in his place before Gorilla came in with a huge lot of ripe fruit, and after making himself comfortable on his haunches with a great bunch before him he rocked himself to and fro, saying while he munched :

" Ha, ha ! Now I have plenty again, and I shall eat it all myself. Ha, ha ! "

" Ha, ha," echoed a thin voice again, so close and clear it seemed to him, that leaping up he made sure to catch it. As there appeared to be no one in the house, he rushed out raging, champing his teeth, and searched the other houses, but meantime Kinneneh carried the bananas to the loft of the gorilla's house, and covered them with barkcloth.

In a short time Gorilla returned furious and disappointed, and sat down to finish the breakfast he had only begun, but on putting out his hands he found only the withered peelings of yesterday's bananas. He looked and rummaged about, but there was positively nothing left to eat. He was now terribly hungry and angry, and he bounded out to obtain another supply, which he brought in and flung on the floor, saying,

" Ha, ha ! I will now eat the whole at once—all to myself, and that other thing which says ' Ha, ha !' after me, I will hunt and mash him like this," and he seized a ripe banana and squeezed it with his paw with so much force that the pulp was squirted all over him. " Ha, ha !" he cried.

" Ha, ha !" mocked the shrill voice, so clear that it appeared to come from behind his ear.

This was too much to bear ; Gorilla bounded up and vented a roar of rage. He tossed the pots, the baskets, the bodies, and bed-grass about— bellowing so loudly and funnily in his fury that Kinneneh, away up in the loft, could scarcely forbear imitating him. But the mocker could not be found, and Gorilla roared loudly in the open place before the village, and tore in and out of each house, looking for him.

Kinneneh descended swiftly from his hiding-place, and bore every banana into the loft as before.

Gorilla hastened to the plantation again, and so angry was he that he uprooted the banana-stalks by the root, and snapped off the clusters with one stroke of his great dog-teeth, and having got together a large stock, he bore it in his arms to the house.

"There," said he, "ha, ha! Now I shall eat in comfort and have a long sleep afterwards, and if that fellow who mocks me comes near—ah! I would—" and he crushed a big bunch in his arms and cried, "ha, ha!"

"Ha, ha! Ha, ha!" cried the mocking voice; and again it seemed to be at the back of his head. Whereupon Gorilla flung his arms behind in the hope of catching him, but there was nothing but his own back, which sounded like a damp drum with the stroke.

"Ha, ha! · Ha, ha!" repeated the voice, at which Gorilla shot out of the door, and raced round the house, thinking that the owner was flying before him, but he never could overtake the flier. Then he went around outside of the other houses, and flew round and round the village, but he could discover naught. But meanwhile Kinneneh had borne all the stock of bananas up into the loft above, and when Gorilla returned there was not one banana of all the great pile he had brought left on the floor.

When, after he was certain that there was not a single bit of a banana left for him to eat, he scratched his sides and his legs, and putting his hand on the top of his head, he uttered a great cry just like a great, stupid child, but the crying did not fill his tummy. No, he must have bananas for that—and he rose up after awhile and went to procure some more fruit.

But when he had brought a great pile of it and had sat down with his nice-smelling bunch before him, he would exclaim, " Ha, ha ! Now—now I shall eat and be satisfied. I shall fill myself with the sweet fruit, and then lie down and sleep. Ha, ha !"

Then instantly the mocking voice would cry out after him, " Ha, ha !" and sometimes it sounded close to his ears, and then behind his head, some-times it appeared to come from under the bananas and sometimes from the doorway, that Gorilla would roar in fury, and he would grind his teeth just like two grinding-stones, and chatter to him-

self, and race about the village, trying to discover
whence the voice came, but in his absence the fruit
would be swept away by his invisible enemy, and
when he would come in to finish his meal, lo! there

"HE WOULD ROAR IN FURY, AND RACE ABOUT THE VILLAGE."

were only blackened and stained banana peelings—
the refuse of his first feast.

Gorilla would then cry like a whipped child, and
would go again into the plantation, to bring some

more fruit into the house, but when he returned with it he would always boast of what he was going to do, and cry out " Ha, ha ! " and instantly his unseen enemy would mock him and cry " Ha, ha ! " and he would start up raving and screaming in rage, and search for him, and in his absence his bananas would be whisked away. And Gorilla's hunger grew on him, until his paunch became like an empty sack, and what with his hunger and grief and rage, and furious raving and racing about, his strength was at last quite exhausted, and the end of him was that on the fifth day he fell from weakness across the threshold of the chief's house, which he had chosen to make his nest, and there died.

When the people of the next village heard of how Kinneneh, a little boy, had conquered the man-killing gorilla, they brought him and his mother away, and they gave him a fine new house and a plantation, and male and female slaves to tend it, and when their old king died, and the period of mourning for him was over, they elected wise Kinneneh to be king over them.

" Ah, friends," said Safeni to his companions, after Kadu had concluded his story, " there is no doubt that the cunning of a son of man prevails over the strongest brute, and it is well for us,

Mashallah ! that it should be so ; for if the elephant, or the lion, or the gorilla possessed but cunning equal to their strength, what would become of us ! "

And each man retired to his hut, congratulating himself that he was born a man-child, and not a thick, muddle-headed beast.

THE CITY OF THE ELEPHANTS.

"MASTER," said Kassim, one of the Basoko boys, "Baruti's tales have brought back from among forgotten things a legend I once knew very well. Ah, I wish I could remember more, but little by little the stories that I used to hear in my childhood from my mother and the old woman who would come and sit with her, will perhaps return again into the mind. I should never have thought of this that I am about to repeat to you now had it not been that Baruti's legends seem to recall as though they were but yesterday the days that came and went uncounted in our Basoko village. This legend is about the City of the Elephants that one of my countrymen and his wife came across in the far past time, in the manner that I shall tell you."

A Bungandu man named Dudu, and his wife
Salimba, were one day seeking in the forest
a long way from the town for a proper red-
wood-tree, out of which they could make a
wooden mortar wherein they could pound their
manioc. They saw several trees of this kind as
they proceeded, but after examining one, and
then another, they would appear to be dis-
satisfied, and say, "Perhaps if we went a little
further on we might find a still better tree for
our purpose."

And so Dudu and Salimba proceeded further
and further into the tall and thick woods, and
ever before them there appeared to be still finer
trees which would after all be unsuited for their
purpose, being too soft, or too hard, or hollow, or
too old, or of another kind than the useful redwood.
They strayed in this manner very far. In the
forest where there is no path or track, it is not
easy to tell which direction one came from, and
as they had walked round many trees, they were
too confused to know which way they ought to
turn homeward. When Dudu said he was sure
that his course was the right one for home,
Salimba was as sure that the opposite was the
true way. They agreed to walk in the direction
Dudu wished, and after a long time spent on it,

they gave it up and tried another, but neither took them any nearer home.

The night overtook them and they slept at the foot of a tree. The next day they wandered still farther from their town, and they became anxious and hungry. As one cannot see many yards off on any side in the forest, an animal hears the coming step long before the hunter gets a chance to use his weapon. Therefore, though they heard the rustle of the flying antelope, or wild pig as it rushed away, it only served to make their anxiety greater. And the second day passed, and when night came upon them they were still hungrier.

Towards the middle of the third day, they came into an open place by a pool frequented by Kiboko (hippo), and there was a margin of grass round about it, and as they came in view of it, both at the same time sighted a grazing buffalo.

Dudu bade his wife stand behind a tree while he chose two of his best and sharpest arrows, and after a careful look at his bow-string, he crept up to the buffalo, and drove an arrow home as far as the guiding leaf which nearly buried it in the body. While the beast looked around and started from the twinge within, Dudu shot his second arrow into his windpipe, and it fell to the ground quite choked. Now here was water to drink and food to eat, and after cutting a load of meat they chose a thick bush-clump a little distance from the pool, made a fire, and, after satisfying their hunger, slept in content. The fourth day they stopped

DUDU AND HIS WIFE MEET A YOUNG LION.

and roasted a meat provision that would last many days, because they knew that luck is not constant in the woods.

On the fifth they travelled, and for three days more they wandered. They then met a young lion who, at the sight of them boldly advanced, but Dudu sighted his bow, and sent an arrow into his chest which sickened him of the fight, and he turned and fled.

A few days afterwards, Dudu saw an elephant standing close to them behind a high bush, and whispered to his wife :

" Ah, now, we have a chance to get meat enough for a month."

" But," said Salimba, " why should you wish to kill him, when we have enough meat still with us ? Do not hurt him. Ah, what a fine back he has, and how strong he is. Perhaps he would carry us home."

" How could an elephant understand our wishes ? " asked Dudu.

" Talk to him anyhow, perhaps he will be clever enough to understand what we want."

Dudu laughed at his wife's simplicity, but to please her he said, " Elephant, we have lost our way, will you carry us and take us home, and we shall be your friends for ever."

The Elephant ceased waving his trunk, and nodding to himself, and turning to them said—

" If you come near to me and take hold of my ears, you may get on my back, and I will carry you safely."

When the Elephant spoke, Dudu fell back from

surprise, and looked at him as though he had not heard aright, but Salimba advanced with all confidence, and laid hold of one of his ears, and pulled herself up on to his back. When she was seated, she cried out, " Come, Dudu, what are you looking at? Did you not hear him say he would carry you?"

Seeing his wife smiling and comfortable on the Elephant's back, Dudu became a little braver and moved forward slowly, when the Elephant spoke again, " Come, Dudu, be not afraid. Follow your wife, and do as she did, and then I will travel home with you quickly."

Dudu then put aside his fears, and his surprise, and seizing the Elephant's ear, he ascended and seated himself by his wife on the Elephant's back.

Without another word the Elephant moved on rapidly, and the motion seemed to Dudu and Salimba most delightful. Whenever any overhanging branch was in the way, the Elephant wrenched it off, or bent it and passed on. No creek, stream, gulley, or river, stopped him, he seemed to know exactly the way he should go, as if the road he was travelling was well known to him.

When it was getting dark he stopped and asked his

friends if they would not like to rest for the night, and finding that they so wished it, he stopped at a nice place by the side of the river, and they slid to the ground, Dudu first, and Salimba last. He then broke dead branches for them, out of which they made a fire, and the Elephant stayed by them, as though he was their slave.

Hearing their talk, he understood that they would like to have something better than dried meat to eat, and he said to them, " I am glad to know your wishes, for I think I can help you. Bide here a little, and I will go and search."

About the middle of the night he returned to them with something white in his trunk, and a young antelope in front of him. The white thing was a great manioc root, which he dropped into Salimba's lap.

" There, Salimba," he said, " there is food for you, eat your fill and sleep in peace, for I will watch over you."

Dudu and Salimba had seen many strange things that day, but they were both still more astonished at the kindly and intelligent care which their friend the Elephant took of them. While they roasted their fresh meat over the flame, and the manioc root was baking under the heap of hot embers, the Elephant dug with his tusks for the juicy roots of his favourite trees round about their camp, and munched away contentedly.

The next morning, all three, after a bathe in the river, set out on their journey more familiar with one another, and in a happier mood.

About noon, while they were resting during the heat of the day, two lions came near to roar at them, but when Dudu was drawing his bow at one of them, the Elephant said :

" You leave them to me ; I will make them run pretty quick," saying which he tore off a great bough of a tree, and flourishing this with his trunk, he trotted on the double quick towards them, and used it so heartily that they both skurried away with their bellies to the ground, and their hides shrinking and quivering out of fear of the great rod.

In the afternoon the Elephant and his human friends set off again, and some time after they came to a wide and deep river. He begged his friends to descend while he tried to find out the shallowest part. It took him some time to do this ; but, having discovered a ford where the water was not quite over his back, he returned to them, and urged them to mount him as he wished to reach home before dark.

As the Elephant was about to enter the river,

he said to Dudu, "I see some hunters o own kind creeping up towards us. Perhaps are your kinsmen. Talk to them, and let us see whether they be friends or foes."

Dudu hailed them, but they gave no answer, and, as they approached nearer, they were seen to prepare to cast their spears, so the Elephant said, "I see that they are not your friends; therefore, as I cross the river, do you look out for them, and keep them at a distance. If they come to the other side of the river, I shall know how to deal with them."

They got to the opposite bank safely; but, as they were landing, Dudu and Salimba noticed that their pursuers had discovered a canoe, and that they were pulling hard after them. But the Elephant soon after landing came to a broad path smoothed by much travel, over which he took them at a quick pace, so fast, indeed, that the pursuers had to run to be able to keep up with them. Dudu, every now and then let fly an arrow at the hunters, which kept them at a safe distance.

Towards night they came to the City of the Elephants, which was very large and fit to shelter such a multitude as they now saw. Their elephant did not linger, however, but took his friends at the same quick pace until they came to a mighty elephant that was much larger than any other, and his ivories were gleaming white and curled up, and exceedingly long. Before him Dudu and Salimba were told by their friend to descend and Salaam, and he told his lord how he had found them lost in the woods, and how for the sake of the kindly words of the woman he had befriended them, and assisted them to the city of his tribe. When the King Elephant heard all this he was much pleased, and said to Dudu and Salimba that they were welcome to his city, and how they should not want for anything, as long as they would be pleased to stay with them, but as for the hunters who had dared to chase them, he would give orders at once. Accordingly he gave a signal, and ten active young elephants dashed out of the city, and in a short time not one of the hunters was left alive, though one of them had leaped into the river, thinking that he could escape in that manner. But then, you know, an elephant is as much at home in a river, as a Kiboko,* so that the last man was soon caught and was drowned.

Dudu and Salimba, however, on account of Salimba's kind heart in preventing her husband wounding the elephant, was made free of the place,

* A hippopotamus.

DUDU AND SALIMBA INTRODUCED TO KING ELEPHANT.

and their friend took them with him to many families, and the big pa's and ma's told their little babies all about them and their habits, and said that, though most of the human kind were very stupid and wicked, Dudu and Salimba were very good, and putting their trunks into their ears they whispered that Salimba was the best of the two. Then the little elephants gathered about them and trotted by their side and around them and diverted them with their antics, their races, their wrestlings, and other trials of strength, but when they became familiar and somewhat rude in their rough play, their elephant friend would admonish them, and if that did not suffice, he would switch them soundly.

The City of the Elephants was a spacious and well-trodden glade in the midst of a thick forest, and as it was entered one saw how wisely the elephant families had arranged their manner of life. For without, the trees stood as thick as water-reeds, and the bush or underwood was like an old hedge of milkweed knitted together by thorny vines and snaky climbers into which the human hunter might not even poke his nose without hurt. Well, the burly elephants had, by much uprooting, created deep hollows, or recesses, wherein a family of two and more might snugly rest, and not even a dart of sunshine might reach them. Round about the great glade the dark leafy arches ran, and Dudu and his wife saw that the elephant families were numerous—for by one sweeping look they could tell that there were more elephants than there are human beings in a goodly village. In some of the recesses there was a row of six and more elephants ; in another the parents stood head to head, and their children, big and little, clung close to their parents' sides ; in another a family stood with heads turned towards the entrance, and so on all around—while under a big tree in the middle there was quite a gathering of big fellows, as though they were holding a serious palaver ; under another tree one seemed to be on the outlook ; another paced slowly from side to side ; another plucked at this branch or at that ; another appeared to be heaving a tree, or sharpening a blunted ivory ; others seemed appointed to uproot the sprouts, lest the glade might become choked with underwood. Near the entrance on both sides was a brave company of them, faces turned outward, swinging their trunks, flapping their ears, rubbing against each other, or who with pate against pate seemed to be drowsily considering something. There was a continual coming in and a going out, singly, or in small companies. The roads that ran through the glade were like a network, clean and smooth, while that which went towards the king's place was so wide that twenty men might walk abreast. At the far end the king stood under his own tree, with his family under the leafy arches behind him.

This was the City of the Elephants as Dudu and Salimba saw it. I ought to say that the outlets of it were many. One went straight through the woods in a line up river, at the other end it ran in a line following the river downward; one went to a lakelet, where juicy plants and reeds throve like corn in a man's fields, and where the elephants rejoiced in its cool waters and washed themselves and infants; another went to an ancient clearing where the plantain and manioc grew wild, and wherein more than two human tribes might find food for countless seasons.

Then said their friend to Dudu and Salimba—

"Now that I have shown you our manner of life, it is for you to ease your longing for awhile and rest with us. When you yearn for home, go tell our king, and he will send you with credit to your kindred."

Then Dudu and his wife resolved to stay, and eat, and they stayed a whole season, not only unhurt, but tenderly cared for, with never a hungry hour or uneasy night. But at last Salimba's heart remembered her children, and kinsfolk, and her own warm house and village pleasures, and on hinting of these memories to her husband, he said that after all there was no place like Bungandu. He remembered his long pipe, and the talk-house, the stool-making, shaft-polishing, bow-fitting, and the little tinkering jobs, the wine-trough, and the merry drinking-bouts, and he wept softly as he thought of them.

They thus agreed that it was time for them to travel homeward, and together they sought the elephant king, and frankly told him of their state.

" My friends," he replied, " be no longer sad, but haste to depart. With the morning's dawn guides shall take you to Bungandu with such gifts as shall make you welcome to your folk. And when you come to them, say to them that the elephant king desires lasting peace and friendship with them. On our side we shall not injure their plantations, neither a plantain, nor a manioc root belonging to them ; and on your side dig no pits for our unwary youngsters, nor hang the barbed iron aloft, nor plant the poisoned stake in the path, so we shall escape hurt and be unprovoked. And Dudu put his hand on the King's trunk as the pledge of good faith.

In the morning, four elephants, as bearers of the

gifts from the king—bales of bark-cloth, and showy mats, and soft hides and other things—and two fighting elephants besides their old friend, stood by the entrance to the city, and when the king elephant came up he lifted Salimba first on the back of their old companion, and then placed Dudu by her side, and at a parting wave the company moved on.

In ten days they reached the edge of the plantation of Bungandu, and the leader halted. The bales were set down on the ground, and then their friend asked of Dudu and his wife—

" Know you where you are ? "

" We do," they answered.

" Is this Bungandu ? " he asked.

" This is Bungandu," they replied.

" Then here we part, that we may not alarm your friends. Go now your way, and we go our way. Go tell your folk how the elephants treat their friends, and let there be peace for ever between us."

The elephants turned away, and Dudu and Salimba, after hiding their wealth in the underwood, went arm in arm into the village of Bungandu. When their friends saw them, they greeted them as we would greet our friends whom we have long believed to be dead, but who come back smiling and rejoicing to us. When the people heard their story they greatly wondered and doubted, but when Dudu and Salimba took them to the place of parting and showed them the prints of seven elephants on the road, and the bales that they had hidden in the underwood, they believed their story. And they made it a rule from that day that no man of the tribe ever should lift a spear, or draw a bow, or dig a pit, or plant the poisoned stake in the path, or hang the barbed iron aloft, to do hurt to an elephant. And as a proof that I have but told the truth go ask the Bungandu, and they will say why none of their race will ever seek to hurt the elephant, and it will be the same as I have told you. That is my story.

THE SEARCH FOR THE HOME OF THE SUN.

WE had a man named Kanga with us in 1883, which name seems to have been bestowed on him by some Islamised resident of Nyangwé by reason of some fancied suggestion made by some of his facial marks to the spots on a guinea-fowl. Kanga had not spoken as yet by the evening fire, but had been an amused listener. When the other tale-tellers were seen sporting their gay robes on the Sunday, it may have inspired him to make an effort to gain one for himself; anyhow, he surprised us one night by saying that he knew of a tale which perhaps we would like to hear. As Kanga's tribe was the

Wasongora-Meno on the right bank of the Lualaba, between Nyangwé and Stanley Falls, the mere mention of a tale from that region was sufficent to kindle my interest.

After a few suitable compliments to Kanga, which were clearly much appreciated, he spoke as follows :

Master and friends. We have an old phrase among us which is very common. It is said that he who waits and waits for his turn, may wait too long, and lose his chance. My tongue is not nimble like some, and my words do not flow like the deep river. I am rather like the brook which is fretted by the stones in its bed, and I hope after this explanation you will not be too impatient with me.

My tale is about King Masama and his tribe, the Balira, who dwelt far in the inmost region, behind (east) us, who throng the banks of the great river. They were formerly very numerous, and many of them came to live among us, but one day King Masama and the rest of the tribe left their country and went eastward, and they have never been heard of since, but those who chose to stay with us explained their disappearance in this way.

A woman, one cold night, after making up her

fire on the hearth, went to sleep. In the middle of the night the fire had spread, and spread, and began to lick up the litter on the floor, and from the litter it crept to her bed of dry banana leaves, and in a little time shot up into flames. When the woman and her husband were at last awakened by the heat, the flames had already mounted into

"THE VILLAGE WAS ENTIRELY BURNED."

the roof, and were burning furiously. Soon they broke through the top and leaped up into the night, and a gust of wind came and carried the long flames like a stream of fire towards the neighbouring huts, and in a short time the fire had caught hold of every house, and the village was entirely burned. It was soon known that besides burning up their houses and much property, several old people and infants had been destroyed by the fire, and the people were horror-struck and angry.

Then one voice said, "We all know in whose house the fire began, and the owner of it must make our losses good to us."

The woman's husband heard this and was alarmed, and guiltily fled into the woods.

In the morning a council of the elders was held, and it was agreed that the man in whose house the fire commenced should be made to pay for his carelessness, and they forthwith searched for him. But when they sought for him he could not be found. Then all the young warriors who were cunning in wood-craft, girded and armed themselves, and searched for the trail, and when one of them had found it, he cried out, and the others gathered themselves about him and took it up, and when many eyes were set upon it, the trail could not be lost.

They soon came up to the man, for he was seated under a tree, bitterly weeping.

Without a word they took hold of him by the arms and bore him along with them, and brought him before the village fathers. He was not a common man by any means. He was known as one of Masama's principal men, and one whose advice had been often followed.

" Oh," said everybody, " he is a rich man, and well able to pay ; yet, if he gives all he has got, it will not be equal to our loss."

The fathers talked a long time over the matter, and at last decided that to save his forfeited life he should freely turn over to them all his property. And he did so. His plantation of bananas and plantains, his plots of beans, yams, manioc, potatoes, ground-nuts, his slaves, spears, shields, knives, paddles and canoes. When he had given up all, the hearts of the people became softened towards him, and they forgave him the rest.

After the elder's property had been equally divided among the sufferers by the fire, the people gained new courage, and set about rebuilding their homes, and before long they had a new village, and they had made themselves as comfortable as ever.

Then King Masama made a law, a very severe law—to the effect that, in future, no fire should be lit in the houses during the day or night ; and the people, who were now much alarmed about fire, with one heart agreed to keep the law. But it was soon felt that the cure for the evil was as cruel as the fire had been. For the houses had been thatched with green banana leaves, the timbers were green and wet with their sap, the floor was damp and cold, the air was deadly, and the people began to suffer from joint aches, and their knees were stiff, and the pains travelled from one place to another through their bodies. The village was filled with groaning.

Masama suffered more than all, for he was old. He shivered night and day, and his teeth chattered sometimes so that he could not talk, and after that his head would burn, and the hot sweat would pour from him, so that he knew no rest.

Then the king gathered his chiefs and principal men together, and said:

"Oh, my people, this is unendurable, for life is with me now but one continuous ague. Let us leave this country, for it is bewitched, and if I stay longer there will be nothing left of me. Lo, my joints are stiffened with my disease, and my muscles are withering. The only time I feel a little ease is when I lie on the hot ashes without the house, but when the rains fall I must needs withdraw indoors, and there I find no comfort, for the mould spreads everywhere. Let us hence at once to seek a warmer clime. Behold whence the sun issues daily in the morning, hot and glowing; there, where his home is, must be warmth, and we shall need no fire. What say you?"

Masama's words revived their drooping spirits.

They looked towards the sun as they saw him mount the sky, and felt his cheering glow on their naked breasts and shoulders, and they cried with one accord : " Let us hence, and seek the place whence he comes."

And the people got ready and piled their belongings in the canoes, and on a certain day they left their village and ascended their broad river, the Lira. Day after day they paddled up the stream, and we heard of them from the Bafanya as they passed by their country, and the Bafanya heard of them for a long distance up— from the next tribe—the Bamoru—and the Bamoru heard about them arriving near the Mountain Land beyond.

Not until a long time afterwards did we hear what became of Masama and his people.

It was said that the Balira, when the river had become shallow and small, left their canoes and travelled by land among little hills, and after winding in and out amongst them they came to the foot of the tall mountain which stands like a grandsire amongst the smaller mountains. Up the sides of the big mountain they straggled, the stronger and more active of them ahead, and as the days passed, they saw that the world was cold and dark until the sun showed himself over the edge of the big mountain, when the day became more agreeable, for the heat pierced into their very marrows, and made their hearts rejoice. The greater the heat became, the more certain were they that they were drawing near the home of the sun. And so they pressed on and on, day after day, winding along one side of the mountain, and then turning to wind again still higher. Each day, as they advanced towards the top, the heat became greater and greater. Between them and the sun there was now not the smallest shrub or leaf, and it became so fiercely hot that finally not a drop of sweat was left in their bodies. One day, when not a cloud was in the sky, and the world was all below them—far down like a great buffalo hide—the sun came out over the rim of the mountain like a ball of fire, and the nearest of them to the top were dried like a leaf over a flame, and those who were behind were amazed at its burning force, and felt, as he sailed over their heads, that it was too late for them to escape. Their skins began to shrivel up and crackle, and fall off, and none of those who were high up on the mountain side were left alive. But a few of those who were nearest the bottom, and the forest belts, managed to take shelter, and remaining there until night, they took advantage of the darkness, when the sun sleeps, to fly from the home of the sun. Except a few poor old people and toddling children, there was none left of the once populous tribe of the Balira.

That is my story. We who live by the great river have taken the lesson, which the end of this tribe has been to us, close to our hearts, and it is this. Kings who insist that their wills should be followed, and never care to take counsel with their people, are as little to be heeded as children who babble of what they cannot know, and therefore in our villages we have many elders who take all matters from the chief and turn them over in their minds, and when they are agreed, they give the doing of them to the chief who can act only as the elders decree.

A HOSPITABLE GORILLA.

"SIR," said Baruti, after we had all gathered around the evening fire, and were waiting expectant for the usual story, "Kassim's tale about the City of the Elephants and the peace that was entered into between the elephants and the Bungandu has reminded me of what happened between a tribe living on the banks of the little Black River above the Basoko, and a Gorilla."

"Wallahi, but these Basoko boys beat everybody for telling stories," exclaimed a Zanzibari. "I wonder, however, whether they invent them, or they really have heard them from their old folk, as they say they did."

" We heard them of course," replied Baruti, with an indignant look; " for how could Kassim or I imagine such things? I heard something each day almost from the elders, or the old women of the tribe. My mother also told me some, and my big brother told me others. At our village talk-house, scarcely a day passed but we heard of some strange thing which had happened in old times. It is this custom of meeting around the master's fire, and the legends that we hear, that reminds us of what we formerly heard, and by thinking and thinking over them the words come back anew to us."

" But do you think these things of which you talk are true?" the Zanzibari asked.

" True!" he echoed. " Who am I that I should say, This thing is true, and that is false! I but repeat what my betters said. I do not speak of what I saw, but of what I heard, and the master's words to us were: ' Try and remember what was said to you in your villages by the ancients among your people, and if you will tell it to me properly, I will give you a nice cloth.' Well, when our old men were in good-humour, and smoked their long pipes, and the pot of wine was by their side, and we asked them to tell us somewhat about the days when they were young, they would say, ' Listen to this now,' and they would tell us of what happened long ago. It is the things of long ago that we remember best, because they were so strange that they clung to the mind, and would not altogether be forgotten. If there is aught unpleasing in them, it is not our fault, for we but repeat the words that entered into our ears."

"That will do, Baruti ; go on with your story ; and you, Baraka, let your tongue sleep," cried Zaidi.

"I but asked a question. Ho ! how impatient you fellows are ! "

"Nay, this is but chatter—we shall never hear the story at this rate. Hyah! Barikallah!* Baruti."

"Well," began Baruti, "this tribe dwelt on the banks of the Black River just above Basoko town, and at that time of the far past the thick forest round about them was haunted by many monstrous animals ; big apes, chimpanzees, gorillas and such creatures, which are not often seen nowadays. Not far from the village, in a darksome spot where the branches met overhead and formed a thick screen, and the lower wood hedged it closely round about so that a tortoise could scarcely penetrate it, there lived the Father of the Gorillas. He had housed himself in the fork of one of the tallest

* Hurry on, in God's name !

trees, and many men had seen the nest as they passed by, but none as yet had seen the owner.

But one day a fisherman in search of rattans to make his nets, wandered far into the woods, and in trying to recover the direction home struck the Black River high up. As he stood wondering whether this was the black stream that flowed past his village, he saw, a little to the right of him, an immense gorilla, who on account of the long dark fur on his chest appeared to be bigger than he really was. A cold sweat caused by his great fear began to come out of the man, and his knees trembled so that he could hardly stand, but when he perceived that the gorilla did not move, but continued eating his bananas, he became comforted a little, and his senses came back. He turned his head around, in order to see the clearest way for a run; but as he was about to start, he saw that the gorilla's eyes were fixed upon him. Then the gorilla broke out into speech and said :

" Come to me, and let me look at thee."

The fisherman's fear came back to him, but he did as he was told, and when he thought he was near enough, he stood still.

Then the gorilla said :

" If thou art kin to me, thou art safe from harm ;

if not, thou canst not pass. How many fingers hast thou ? " he asked.

" Four," the fisherman answered, and he held a hand up with its back towards the gorilla, and his thumb was folded in on the palm so that it could not be seen by the beast.

" Aye—true indeed. Why, thou must be a kinsman of ours, though thy fur is somewhat scanty. Sit down and take thy share of this food, and eat."

The fisherman sat down, and broke off bananas from the stalk and ate heartily.

" Now mind," said the gorilla, " thou hast eaten food with me. Shouldst thou ever meet in thy wanderings any of my brothers, thou must be kind to them in memory of this day. Our tribe has no quarrel with any of thine, and thy tribe must have none against any of mine. I live alone far down this river, and thy tribe lives further still. Mind our password, ' *Tu-wheli*, *Tu-wheli*.' By that we know who is friendly and who is against us."

The fisherman departed, and speeding on his way reached his village safely ; but he kept secret what he had seen and met that day.

Some little time after, the tribe resolved to have a grand hunt around their village, to scare the beasts of the forest away ; for in some things they resemble us. If we leave a district undisturbed for a moon or so, the animals think that we have either departed the country or are afraid of them. The apes and the elephants are the worst in that respect, and always lead the way, pressing on our heels, and often sending their scouts ahead to report, or as a hint to us that we are lingering too long.

The people loaded themselves with their great nets, and first chose the district where the Gorilla Father lived. They set their nets around a wide space, and then the beaters were directed to make a large sweep and drive all the game towards the nets, and here and there where the netting was weak, the hunters stood behind a thick bush, their heavy spears ready for the fling.

Well, it just happened that at that very time the Father of the Gorillas was holding forth to his kinsmen, and the first they knew of the hunt, and that a multitude of men were in the woods, was when they heard the horrid yells of the beaters, the sound of horns, the jingle of iron, and the all-round swish of bushes.

The fisherman, like the rest of his friends, was well armed, and he was as keen as the others for the hunt, but soon after he heard the cries of the beaters, he saw a large gorilla rushing out of the bushes, and knew him instantly for his friend, and he cried out "*Tu-wheli! Tu-wheli!*" At the sound of it the gorilla led his kinsmen towards him, and passed the word to those behind, saying, "Ah, this is our friend. Do not hurt him."

The gorillas passed in a long line of mighty fellows, close by the fisherman, and as they heard the voice of their father, they only whispered to him, "*Tu-wheli, Tu-wheli*," but the last of all was a big, sour-faced gorilla, who, when he saw that the pass was only guarded by one man, made a rush at him. His roar of rage was heard by the father, and turning back he knew that his human brother was in danger, and he cried out to those nearest to part them, "The man is our brother;" but as the fierce gorilla was deaf to words, the father loped back to them, and slew him, and then hastened away as the hunters were pressing up.

These, when they came up and observed that the fisherman's spear was still in his hand, and not painted with blood, were furious, and they agreed together that he should not have a share of the meat, "For," said they, "he must have been in a league against us." Neither did he obtain any share of the spoil.

A few days after this the fisherman was proceeding through a part of the forest, and a gorilla met him in the path, and said :

"Stay, I seem to know thee. Art thou not our brother?"

"*Tu-wheli, Tu-wheli!*" he cried.

"Ah, it is true, follow me;" and they went together to the gorilla's nesting-tree, where the fisherman was feasted on ripe bananas, berries, and nuts, and juicy roots, and he was shown which roots and berries were sweet, and which were bitter, and so great was the variety of food he saw, that he came to know that though lost in the forest a wise man need not starve.

When the fisherman returned to his village he called the elders together, and he laid the whole story of his adventures before his people, and when the elders heard that the berries and roots, nuts, and mushrooms in the forest, of which they had hitherto been afraid, were sweet and wholesome, they exclaimed with one voice, that the gorillas had proved themselves true friends, and had given them much useful knowledge; and it was agreed among them that in future the gorillas should be reckoned among those, against whom it would not be lawful to raise their spears.

Ever since the tribes on the Black River avoid harming the gorilla, and all his kind big and little; neither will any of the gorilla trespass on their plantations, or molest any of the people.